PICTURE

Jen

MW00930937

JENNA ST. JAMES BOOKS

Ryli Sinclair Mystery Series (cozy)

Picture Perfect Murder   *Bachelorettes and Bodies*
Girls' Night Out Murder   *Rings, Veils, and Murder*
Old-Fashioned Murder   *Next Stop Murder*
Bed, Breakfast & Murder   *Gold, Frankincense & a Merry Murder*
Veiled in Murder   *Heartache, Hustle, & Homicide*

Sullivan Sisters Mystery Series (cozy)

Murder on the Vine   *PrePEAR to Die*
Burning Hot Murder   *Tea Leaves, Jealousy, & Murder*

Copper Cove Mystery Series (cozy)

Seaside & Homicide

A Witch in Time Series (paranormal)

Time After Time
Runaway Bride Time (novella)

A Trinity Falls Series (romantic comedy)

Blazing Trouble
Cougar Trouble

DEDICATION

To my mom, Sue Buhman, thank you for always encouraging me to follow my dreams.

To my sister, Juliana Buhman, thank you for helping me with book covers, edits, and ideas.

To James, thank you for standing by me and reminding me I could make a living writing.

CHAPTER 1

I hate looking at dead bodies. And believe me, I've seen a lot of them in my twenty-eight years. There's nothing that can prepare you for that first glimpse of death.

In college, I worked part time at Jaworski Funeral Home. It was one of those small, family-owned businesses. They were great about working around my class schedule. They were even better about including me as family. A few holiday dinners and family gatherings later, and Ryli Jo Sinclair had become an honorary Jaworski.

For four years I did everything from flower arranging to consoling families. I didn't deal with the actual prepping of the dead body. But still, a dead body was a dead body as far as I was concerned.

However, tonight was completely different. This dead body wasn't neatly arranged in a silk-lined casket. This dead body was spread out over the kitchen table, naked from the waist up, covered in blood, and missing a heart.

I swallowed and pushed down the bile that rose in my throat. Tonight I was moonlighting as the forensic photographer in my small hometown of Granville, Missouri. Mainly because the newspaper I work for, *The Granville Gazette,* doesn't pay me enough money to survive.

I've worked for *The Gazette,* the one and only newspaper in town, since returning from college six years ago. I graduated with a major in journalism and a minor in photography. A few months later, not only didn't I have a full-time job, but my college loans were coming due. A few desperate weeks after that, my mom called and said *The Gazette* was looking for a reporter and photographer.

So now here I was, stuck in the same small town I'd left, writing fluff pieces for people who make being nosey neighbors an actual art form.

But I like my job. Since the newspaper is small, I not only write the stories, but I also help with layout, editing, and taking photographs.

The Granville Police Department also calls me whenever they need a professional. And tonight they definitely needed me.

"God, what a freaking mess," Officer Troy Chunsey muttered, holding his hand under his nose.

I glanced over at Officer Chunsey. *Nothing like stating the obvious.*

Officer Chunsey was around twenty-four, overweight, and still had a baby face. Although his baby face wasn't looking too good right now. In fact, it had already turned four different colors since we'd arrived in the bloodied kitchen.

"If you're gonna throw up, Chunsey, you'd better do it outside!" Chief Kimble barked.

Garrett Kimble was our new chief of police for Granville. I say new because he's only been here for a little over a year. In order *not* to be new in Granville, you'd have to be born here. Everyone else is considered new in town.

Kimble came to us from the Kansas City Police Department where he worked for almost eight years after leaving active duty.

He has jet-black hair styled short from his military days, and cold blue eyes, also left over from his military days. And did I mention a body that could make a nun weep? I tried staying clear of him when he first came to town…mainly because he makes the spit in my mouth dry up. Whether it's from sheer terror or sexual frustration, I don't know, but more and more lately I've been thinking of finding out.

He's about ten years older than me, give or take a few months. I've never really dated an older guy. Who am I kidding, I've not really dated a whole lot period; so older, younger, I guess it doesn't matter.

Recently I've been not so subtle in my advances toward him. I figure it's better to let him know I'm interested than making him guess. The thing I worry about most is whether or not I can handle a guy like Kimble. There's no doubt in my mind he could chew me up and spit me out before I even know what happened. He's good friends with my older brother, Matt, so we are constantly being thrown together. No doubt about it the chemistry is there.

I looked over at Melvin Collins, the coroner. "Just making the pronouncement. I haven't really had time to do much else, Chief."

"Ryli, get over here with that camera," Chief Kimble ordered.

Walking over to him, I carefully averted my eyes from the table. Not so much out of respect, but because I was afraid I was gonna puke. Then Kimble would be yelling at me instead of Chunsey.

"Start shooting," Chief Kimble said. "Make sure you miss nothing."

6

The body, which was once known as Dr. Vera Garver, stared back at me with empty eyes. I lifted my camera and started shooting. I'd probably taken seven chest shots before I lowered my camera and backed up from the table to really look at her and the crime scene.

Garver probably weighed one hundred sixty pounds and had shoulder-length brown hair, which was currently covered in blood. Actually, everything was pretty much covered in blood.

The oak table that housed her body wasn't really all that big. It was one of those round, kitchen-nook tables. This meant her feet were dangling off the edge. You could tell the chairs had been pushed back quickly because one was toppled over.

I carefully avoided the blood as best I could and walked away from the body toward the main area of the kitchen. The dark brown granite countertops and stainless steel appliances gleamed under the bright lights of the kitchen.

The kitchen was pristine except for the two coffee mugs, two plates, and two forks drying on a dish towel beside the sink. Almost like Dr. Garver had been entertaining right before she died.

This was definitely going to be a hard one to solve. Garver was probably the most hated person in all of Granville. She'd been the superintendent of our local school for almost a decade.

"You know we're gonna have to question the whole town, right?" Chunsey said. "Everyone is pretty much a suspect when it comes to who'd want her dead."

I bit back a chuckle. Just nervous laughter I was sure, since I wasn't used to dealing with such graphic scenes. Truth was, Chunsey was right for once in his life.

I didn't think many people would openly weep for Garver, but I couldn't really think much of anything because the smell was making me light headed.

I lifted my camera and walked back toward the body, again avoiding the blood as best I could.

I glanced down at Garver's fingers, getting ready to snap a picture of her hands, which were also dangling off the table, when I noticed something odd. I squatted down to get a better look.

Okay, now I did gag.

"What's wrong?" Kimble walked over to the corner of the room where I had quickly retreated, still hunched over, taking deep breaths.

I didn't dare say anything for fear of what would come out...or come up. Instead, I pointed to Garver's hands the best I could from my precarious position. Garrett's latex-gloved hand reached down and gently lifted Dr. Garver's right hand. The fatty tips of her fingers had all been cut off.

I just hate it when that happens.

Now I did laugh. Hysterical laughter. Never good when you're trying to be taken seriously.

Ignoring me, Garrett walked around the table to examine her other hand. Same thing.

"Guess the gaping hole in her chest made it easy to overlook," Chunsey muttered.

Kimble's eyes cut to the officer then back at me. "Good job catching it." Kimble gave me one of his rare smiles. I almost felt a little better.

"Why cut off her fingertips?" I asked after getting myself together. "It's not like we'd have to ID the body through fingerprints."

"Not sure," was all Kimble said.

I walked back over to the table and continued snapping pictures of the body, blocking out the images, and just getting lost in the lighting and angles as best I could.

I know most folks would think that being a newspaper journalist and working for the police department might be a conflict of interest, but usually there wasn't anything that interesting to scoop. Besides, like I said, I really needed the extra money. It was nice being able to eat on a regular basis.

Of course, until tonight, most of my jobs for the police department consisted of photographing vehicular accidents, vandalism…that type of thing. Nothing like this.

Working with the police department also let me believe I helped solve cases. I know I wasn't really solving them, but a part of me enjoyed putting clues together and coming up with theories. The other officers on the squad—outside of Kimble—will usually answer the questions I ask them while I shoot.

"I don't see evidence of a struggle," I commented, trying to make conversation.

Stony stare from Kimble.

"I'm just saying. The house isn't trashed, and she doesn't appear to have defensive wounds on her arms or anything."

Again, stony stare. "You are snapping pictures…that's all."

Shrugging, I finished up with the body and went into the living room, snapping pictures just in case. It was a newer house with an open-floor concept. You could be in the kitchen and still watch television in the living room. At the far end of the living room there was a desktop computer, flat screen monitor, and multi-use printer.

Melvin Collins walked back into the room. "I contacted the medical examiner in Brywood. They are expecting the body tonight. Couple days for the autopsy and answers, hopefully."

"Where's the husband?" Kimble asked when he finished with the body.

Officer Chunsey raised his head off the kitchen counter. "He's in the formal dining room. Matt took him in there to get him settled down. Husband's the one that came home and found the body around eleven. Called 911."

"Pretty late night for Mr. Garver, isn't it?" Kimble asked.

"This is Thursday night," I volunteered. Since Kimble just raised his eyebrow at me, I figured I better elaborate. "Professor Garver teaches English at a local college over in Brywood. Everyone knows that Thursday night is his long night. He has class from six to ten."

"Everyone knows?" Kimble said.

"Yeah. It's a small town, in case you forgot." Even to my own ears I sounded defensive. But it was true. The Professor had been teaching that class on Thursday nights for about nine years. He was pretty much a staple. If you wanted to take his class, and you wanted to take it at night, you had to take it on Thursday nights. It was the only night class he had.

"I haven't forgotten." I could tell by the way Kimble glared at me I hadn't heard the end of it. "So he ends class at ten, stays around and gets his papers in order, maybe talks to a student, walks out to his car, then drives home. It's about a thirty-minute drive from Brywood, so that could put him home around eleven. Comes in, sees the body, calls 911. Gives him a nice, solid alibi."

I never did know when to keep my mouth shut. "Please, you don't really think that Professor Garver is capable of this, do you?" I gestured my hand vaguely in the area of Vera Garver's body. I still wasn't fully capable of looking at it without gagging.

"Well, Ms. Sinclair, if not her husband, who do you think we should be looking at? Please enlighten me with one of your theories." I could tell he was pissed, especially since he used my last name. As soon as Kimble started using my last name, I know I've pushed enough and it's time to shut up. So I took the easy way out and shrugged my shoulders.

"Well, seeing as how I'm still the acting chief of police around here, perhaps I'll go in and talk to Professor Garver just the same." He paused and gave me a heated look. "And when you're finished, just wait for me in my office at the station. I'm sure I won't be much longer."

Why couldn't I just keep my mouth shut around him? Probably because he made me so nervous I just couldn't help myself. Now I was going to get chewed out by Kimble.

Truth was, Garrett Kimble has never raised his voice to me personally, but I've heard him chew out others enough to know it could be brutal.

Half an hour later I finished off my last roll of film. I took plenty of pictures because after my run-in with Kimble, I didn't want to take any chances of not getting everything possible. Plus, a few of the other guys on the squad were willing to whisper their theories to me. But mainly, I didn't want to give him an opportunity to fire me. Packing up my gear, I decided to snoop and find out where everyone was.

I walked down the short, spacious hallway that led away from the kitchen and living room. There were several framed pictures lining the two walls. I paused to look at them. Most were of the two adult Garver kids, a boy and a girl, and a granddaughter. I actually felt a twinge of pity for Dr. Garver. She'd never be able to see her family again.

Hearing voices, I turned left and saw Professor Garver sitting on a mocha leather couch, a handkerchief dabbing at his eyes. Kimble sat directly across from him in a matching leather chair. My big brother, Matt, sat next to Professor Garver. He must have sensed my presence like only siblings can because he slowly turned his head and smiled at me.

Matt works as an EMT and part-time firefighter for Granville. He lives in a nice two-story house off Main Street, which he bought about six months ago. I was kind of surprised he'd bought it since he already had a place in town he owned. His purchase was a perk for me, because now he lets me live in his old house.

Matt has been seeing my best friend, Paige, for almost a year now, and neither of us can figure out why he hasn't popped the question. Paige currently lived in a tiny trailer on her parents' land. She helped out at their farm doing the books for her dad and helped her mom when needed. It's a large farm, so she's busy most days.

Paige has been in love with Matt since elementary school. Matt was four years older than us, and Paige was my best friend...needless to say he didn't look twice at her. When he joined

12

the Army, Paige took it almost as hard as I did. She wrote to him in boot camp and then later when he was overseas in Afghanistan. When he'd come home on leave for a few weeks, Paige was always certain he'd ask her out, but he never did. When he finally got out of the military after serving eight years, he decided to live in Kansas City. Paige eventually woke up to the fact that Matt wasn't going to be her happily ever after.

Little did we know what was really going on with Matt. I found out later that the reason he chose to stay in Kansas City was because he suffered from survivor's guilt. And until he got help, he didn't believe he could come back to Granville.

Kansas City was also where Matt first met Chief Kimble. They were both at a veterans' function, and Matt said it was because of Kimble's help that he was able to get through what he needed to and move on with his life.

When the chief of police position came open in Granville, Matt made sure Kimble knew about it and was instrumental in getting his name pushed through. One of the many perks of personally knowing the mayor and city manager in a small town.

Matt met my eyes across the room and gave me a slight nod. I could tell he was taking this hard. Matt was that way. He had a gentle heart underneath his tough exterior. I like to think he got that from our dad. I don't know for sure considering I was just a baby when our dad died in a single-car collision. But my mom always described him as a gentle giant.

I listened to Kimble ask Professor Garver a few questions, but the truth was he didn't seem to know anything. So I decided to head to the station to drop off my film.

I shut the front door of the Garver house and walked briskly to my car. Not so much from the cool October air, but because I was still more shaken than I cared to admit.

I'd parked my car behind the three other vehicles already in the long, curved driveway. The house was about fifty yards from the street, which was also deserted this late at night.

The Garvers technically lived in town, but it was on the outskirts of town, so it had a country feel. The nearest neighbor was probably a quarter of a mile away, and the driveway was lined on both sides with shrubs that were taller than me.

The oak tree in the front yard and all the tall shrubs surrounding the house definitely provided plenty of shade...but also plenty of protection from an intruder being seen.

CHAPTER 2

I pulled into the police station and turned off my car. It was pitch black outside, and it looked even darker inside the station. Usually the darkness didn't bother me, but after what I'd seen tonight, I was more than a little creeped out. Putting on my big-girl panties, I opened the door and took out the camera bag. I rifled through my keychain until I came up with the key to get into the station. Claire, the dispatcher for the graveyard shift, should be inside. Running the last few feet to the door, I unlocked it as fast as my shaking fingers allowed and pushed it open.

"Hello?" a female voice called. "Who's out there?"

"Hey, Claire. It's me, Ryli. I wanted to drop off the rolls of film for Chief Kimble before I went home."

Claire Hickman shuffled into the main room. Claire was in her late fifties, stood about five foot nothing, and was as big around as she was tall. She was always bringing in homemade cookies and cakes for the boys, which was probably why she was as big around as tall. And as far as her clothing style went—let me just say, she never met a crushed velour jogging suit she didn't love. She had tightly curled gray hair that she got styled every week over at Legends Salon and Nails.

Pretty much everyone in town went to Legends for either hair or nails. Or in most cases, the never-ending supply of gossip that found its way between those walls. The owner, Iris Newman, was known to repeat all the latest gossip about everyone in town as she teased hair and buffed nails. Of course there were other hair salons in town, but they weren't nearly as popular.

"Oh, my God. Is it true? Did someone *really* murder Dr. Garver? I just can't believe it. Who would do such a thing? I mean, who hasn't thought about killing that old blowhard…but still, who would actually *do* it?" Claire took a deep breath and closed her eyes. For a minute, I thought she was going to cross herself.

"Well," Claire continued, "it was only a matter of time. You anger the wrong person, and you never know what someone will do. Truth is, between you and me," Claire leaned in, looking over her shoulder as though someone would overhear, "I can't believe her husband stayed with her all these years. He's such a sweet, gentle man."

"Yes, he is."

"Oh, you poor dear," Claire said, patting me on the arm. "You need to get yourself home and have a glass of wine. It always helps me to relax."

"I need to stick around for a minute and talk with Chief Kimble real quick."

"Uh oh, what did you do?" Claire asked.

"Nothing!"

"Tsk-tsk. Girl, when're you gonna learn not to push that man. Garrett Kimble could chew you up and spit you out before you open your mouth to scream."

Wow…hadn't I just thought as much?

"Not that being chewed up by that hunk of a man would be all bad," Claire winked.

I shuddered. "Gross!"

Claire snorted and turned to waddle back into her cubicle to wait for another phone call. "Believe it little girl. I may be getting old, but I'm not dead." Claire stopped and turned. "Hey, speaking of which, you suppose it's too early to call the Professor and maybe see about setting up a date?"

"Yes!"

"You and I both know that twelve other old maids are gonna be swarming that man in no time. I need to make sure I'm there, too." Claire patted her close-cropped curled. "Maybe I should call Iris in the morning and make a hair appointment. I want to look good for the funeral."

Shaking my head, I walked into Garrett's office and started poking around. I'd been in here tons of times, but usually he was in here too, so snooping wasn't practical. The office had white, bare walls, with a beat-up hardwood floor. His desk was made of metal and looked like it had been run over by a tank. He didn't have any pictures or personal items except for a traditional banker's lamp sitting smack dab in the middle of the desk.

I walked over to his built-in bookcase and picked up a wooden box containing a medal. I brushed my hands over it, wondering how he got it. I set it down and picked up the only photograph in the whole place. It was a picture of Garrett in his police uniform. He was in the middle, with one arm draped over a shorter, sandy-haired guy in a similar police uniform, and his other arm draped over a stunning blonde, who smiled into the camera. She didn't have dull, dirty blonde hair like me, but shiny, silky blonde hair that I would kill for. I leaned down for a closer look.

She was almost as tall as Garrett, slim, and beautiful. She had blue-green eyes and nice full lips. In comparison, I'm not all that tall, have more curves than straights, and my eyes aren't two-toned complex orbs, just a simple hazel. Looking at her, I felt ordinary and plain.

Was this woman an old girlfriend or ex-wife? One thing Garrett never did was talk about himself much. I do know that in the year he's been in town, he hasn't dated anyone. I've made it my business to know.

"Are you touching my things, Sin?"

I squealed and whirled around. Unfortunately, I also banged the picture against the bookshelf. I'm always doing stupid, clumsy stuff like that. Instead of answering, I put the picture back where it was. I was stalling. I didn't have the courage to say anything yet.

Finally I turned around. "Nope. Just waiting for you. You *did* tell me to wait in your office, didn't you? Believe me, I'd rather be home right now, trying to forget this night."

For a brief second I thought I saw compassion in his eyes, but it was gone in a flash. Instead of commenting, he shut the door to his office. Great, there weren't any windows, and now he'd shut the only way to escape out of the room. No one could see him throttle me.

"Come here," Garrett said.

I swallowed and tried to look tough as I walked toward him. I didn't say anything but stopped about two feet away from him. He looked dangerous in his tight black jeans and black shirt. Usually he wears a uniform, but since he was at home when he got the call, he obviously just threw on some clothes. He looked magnificent in them, probably even better out of them.

18

"Closer, Sin."

I scowled and leaned in. He *knows* I hate it when he calls me that. How many times did I have to tell the oaf that my last name was *Sinclair*, not *Sin*? I was almost nose-to-chest with him.

He reached out and lifted a curl from my shoulder, winding it around his finger. "Leave the investigating to me."

Of all the things he could have said and done, I was not expecting this. Truth was I didn't know what to say, he'd caught me so off guard.

"I'm serious," Garrett said. "I heard your questions and suppositions back at the house."

"I don't know what you mean," I said, suddenly fixated on a chip in the wall over his right shoulder.

"Yes, you do. This isn't some cute little puzzle to put together…it's a murder. Leave it to the professionals."

I tried to squelch the urge to kick his butt. Mainly because I knew I'd never win.

He turned and walked toward his desk. "It's been a long night. Go home and get some rest. Tomorrow's going to be tough, too. I have to do a follow-up interview with Mr. Garver before he goes to the funeral home, and then I have to start piecing this murder together."

"I dropped off the film for you," I said.

"Appreciate it."

Garrett didn't say anything else, so I turned to leave.

"Hey," Kimble said, "one more thing. Your brother invited me over for dinner tomorrow night. There's no high school football game this week, so I don't have to help control crowds. Anyway, he said if I saw you first, to tell you to come over, too.

We're gonna start grilling steaks around seven." He opened the door for me. "Now, go home. I'll call you tomorrow if I need you. Oh, and Ryli, I know you'll have to write something for the paper, but use discretion, please. I don't want anyone knowing that not only is the heart missing, but so are the fingertips."

I nodded. "I understand."

He gave me a predatory smile. "Let me walk you out to your car."

Usually I would protest being walked to my car like a scared little girl, but since that's how I felt, I said nothing. I called good night to Claire and followed Garrett outside. Neither of us said anything as I opened my door and got into the car. I lifted my hand to wave goodbye. Garrett gave me a small smile and nodded his head.

It only took me a few minutes to drive from the police station to my house. Just one of the many perks of living in a small town.

My house is a one-bedroom, eight hundred square foot cottage. It currently sports a faded yellow exterior with white shutters. I put a window box under my one and only window in the front of the house to give it more personality. The porch spans the front of the house and sags dangerously in some places.

I unlocked my front door and stepped inside. I felt a brush against the bottom of my legs and bent down to pick up Miss Molly. Molls is my black and white longhaired cat. I'd gotten her from the animal shelter here in town right after I moved into the house. I hated coming home to an empty place, so I thought a cat would be the perfect roommate.

And I was right. Miss Molly greets me warmly every time I come home…as long as I remember to stock up on kitty treats and catnip.

Walking into the tiny kitchen to give Miss Molly a treat, I couldn't help but think about what Garrett had said to me. Why on earth would the killer keep the heart and the fingertips? What did they signify?

I mean, the no heart thing was a no-brainer. Anyone who'd met Vera Garver knew she had no heart. So I can see the symbolism of cutting out her heart. But why cut off her fingertips? What on earth could that symbolize?

"Meow."

I bent down to pick Molls up and stroked her fur. Her rhythmic purr calmed me at once. "What's the matter Miss Molly? You scared, too?"

"Meow."

"I know. I'm a little freaked out myself. How about you sleep with me tonight?"

Miss Molly leapt out of my arms and sashayed into the living room. Well, I guess that answered that question. Not that I'm surprised, she hardly ever wants to have anything to do with me. I don't know why I bother.

I changed into sweats and a t-shirt, grabbed a pint of Gelato from the freezer, and sat down on my couch. Maybe the mixture of fantastic Italian ice cream and lack of sleep would give me some ideas for a story.

Twenty minutes later, not only didn't I have a story, but my stomach hurt from all the ice cream I'd blindly shoveled into my mouth. I tossed the empty container and crawled into bed…Miss Molly nowhere in sight. Big surprise there.

CHAPTER 3

I woke up to the sound of vibrations coming from my cell phone. Funny how I thought I might be able to sleep through that little annoyance. No such luck. It was Hank Perkins, owner of *The Gazette*. I was being summoned to the office for a debriefing. It wouldn't have been such a big deal if I'd gone right to sleep last night. Unfortunately, I tossed and turned and actually saw the sunrise before I finally drifted off.

I threw on jeans, a t-shirt, brushed my teeth, and piled my hair on top of my head. Most days when I go to the office, I just throw on whatever is clean...or at least semi-clean. Grabbing my travel mug full of coffee, I threw Miss Molly a kiss and ran out the door.

Granville has a population of just over ten thousand. At least, that's what the sign outside the city limits claims. I've not known that number to change much in the twenty-eight years I've been alive, so who really knows.

The town was made up of two main streets, Elm Street and Pike Street. They met in the heart of downtown at a four-way stop. On the downtown square we have the courthouse, Legends Salon and Nails, a couple banks, Steve's Sub Shop, two café-type restaurants, and a handful of antiques stores. On the outskirts of town going west, we have Burger Barn, the elementary, middle, and high schools, along with a small hospital. On the east side of town we have a small family-run grocery store, the police station, and the newspaper building where I work.

Thrown into this mixture are numerous houses and churches. I've attended the same church that my mom and brother have for about as long as I've been alive. In fact, Pastor Williams and his wife, Sharon, have pastored there for as long as I've been alive—a slight exaggeration, but not by much. Come to think of it, Dr. Garver attended my church and was even on the church board.

It doesn't take more than two minutes for me to get to work, so believe it or not I'm hardly ever late. I pulled into the open slot outside the one-story brick building that housed the newspaper. The staff is basically made up of three people...the owner and editor, Hank, his wife, Mindy, and me.

"About time," Hank grumbled around the unlit cigar in his mouth as I pulled open the glass door and walked in.

"Leave her alone, Hank." Mindy said as she greeted me with a hug. "Can't you see she's had a hard night?"

"I don't care. I have a paper to run. I can't take time out to worry about the princess's lack of beauty sleep."

I narrowed my eyes at him and barely resisted the urge to shoot him the bird. Not that it would have bothered him any, he probably would have shot it right back at me. Or just literally shot me. He's a "Kill 'Em All, Let God Sort 'Em Out" kinda guy. A retired Marine who still walks the walk and talks the talk. Once a Marine, always a Marine. Oorah!

His closely shaved military haircut did little to disguise his bulbous forehead, nor did it help cover his protruding ears. He was fifty-two years old, mean as the day was long, and didn't give two figs about anything but his wife and his paper.

Mindy on the other hand was his opposite in every way. She was as gentle as he was mean. She had platinum blonde hair that was teased for miles, something she never let go of from her Texas pageant days. I don't know her real age, because she won't tell me, but I'm guessing around fifty.

For an older lady, she has a killer body, which she loves to show off. Skin-tight floral pants and neon colored off-the-shoulder shirts or sweaters are her signature, paired with designer five-inch high-heeled shoes. Think Naomi Harper from *Mama's Family*...only way smarter. Thank goodness for Nick at Nite reruns.

"Honey, you just sit down right here and tell me all about it." Mindy handed me a cup of her special blend herbal tea and pushed me into a chair.

The front office was averaged size, had no walls, and was sparsely decorated. When you walked through the glass front doors, you pretty much walked into the whole office. We have a back room where we put the paper together, a small bathroom down the hall, and another tiny closet that Hank used as his office. Mindy and I worked in the front office area, which was fine by me. The less I had to deal with Hank, the better off I was.

Hank thrust his hands in my face. "Let's see it."

"See what?"

"The article. I know you didn't just go home and sleep. Give me the article."

"Are you freaking serious?" I asked. "I didn't get home until after one, and then I had to try and get all that blood out of my head before I could sleep."

"You're telling me you didn't write anything?" Hank demanded. "What the heck do I pay you for?"

I knew better than to answer him, so I just gave him my best "bite me" stare. To a seasoned Marine, I probably just looked like an idiot. But I didn't care. There was no way I could put together a story last night. I took a drink of Mindy's herbal tea and said nothing.

"I want you to get out today and get reactions," Hank demanded. "Go up to Legends. You know Iris is going to be shooting her mouth off. I want specific gut-wrenching reactions from people. Give me lots of quotes!"

"Fine," I said as I walked to my desk. I set the hot tea down and picked up my spiral notebook. I really didn't want to talk with a bunch of gossiping old ladies, but I did want to keep my job. Matt appreciates it when I make his mortgage payments.

* * *

Before I headed to Legends, I made a quick stop. My mom was a retired elementary school teacher. She taught kids in Granville for thirty years before she decided to call it quits. The majority of the younger population in town has gone through Janine Sinclair's classroom at one time or another. Eventually, though, she decided she didn't like the changes being made with the new administration, so she retired.

Mom kept saying she was going to sell the house, and that it's too big and she doesn't need a two-story house. But I don't think she'll ever do it. There are just too many memories. I smelled cinnamon rolls before I entered the spacious kitchen and had already devoured two rolls by the time she walked in.

"I was wondering where you were." Mom leaned down and kissed the top of my head. "It's after eight, and you know I always have cinnamon rolls."

My mom was hands down the best cook around. Unfortunately, that usually meant people thought *I* must be a great cook, too. Like somehow there's a magical cooking gene in DNA that gets passed down through generations. There isn't. I've tried cooking and baking hundreds of recipes, and only a few have been edible.

"So, who do you think did it?" I asked, wiping my mouth with my hand.

"Did what?" Mom asked.

"Hello...murdered Dr. Garver."

"What!"

"Didn't you hear?"

"No, I didn't! I turned my cell off last night." I watched as she continued to wring her hands together in worry. "This is horrible!"

Why Mom thought it was horrible I didn't know. She disliked Dr. Garver as much as anyone. And for Mom, that was a feat. I've never known my mom to dislike anyone, but Dr. Garver was a different matter.

"We just started the new school year," Mom went on. "Where on earth are they going to find someone to fill her spot this late in the game?"

That made more sense. Mom was worried about the school.

"Were you and Matt called to the scene? What happened?"

I didn't know if I should tell her exactly what happened. It was pretty gruesome. Although, if I didn't tell her and she found out later—which she was bound to do—she'd probably turn me over her knee. She liked to think she could still do that.

"Okay. But you have to understand, most of this isn't going to be printed, so you can't repeat this. It looks like someone dragged her into the kitchen, cut out her heart, and chopped of her fingertips."

Mom's mouth dropped open. "You're not serious?"

"I am. I just can't believe you hadn't heard until now."

Mom didn't meet my eyes. "Like I said, I turned off my cell. I was busy—reading. I was reading."

Warning bells went off in my head. Something didn't sound right. "Everything okay?" I tried to keep it casual, but I'm not sure I succeeded.

"Oh, yes. I'm fine," Mom said, waving a hand dismissively. "I take it Matt was with you?"

"Yes. He stayed with Mr. Garver," I said as I took my empty plate to the sink. "Mr. Garver was the one that came home after class and found her."

"That poor man. I always did like him. Never could understand how he came to marry that woman."

Evidently that's the sixty-four thousand dollar question. Well, that and who killed her.

"I'm meeting Paige at Burger Barn this morning to talk. Then I have to go over to Legends to get reactions from people. You know everyone's going to be talking about the murder, and what better place to hear the latest gossip than down there?" Mom nodded her head in agreement. "But before I leave, I was wondering if I can ask a favor?"

"Of course. What is it?"

"Well, Matt invited Garrett, Paige, and me over for dinner tonight, and I want to do something special. I was wondering if I could borrow that chocolate jelly roll recipe you have so I can make a dessert."

Mom didn't say anything for about five seconds. "Do you want me to make it for you?"

"I'm pretty sure I can handle it."

Again, dead silence.

"I can do this," I insisted. "You always said it's one of the easiest things to make."

Mom leaned over and patted my hand, "Of course you can. The recipe's in the box on the shelf next to the stove. Make sure you can read my writing. You know how I just jot things down by hand. Do you need the ingredients?"

"No, thanks. I'll go to the store when I finish up at Legends." Suddenly excited at the prospect of showing off to Garrett, I couldn't sit still. "Thanks again, Mom. I'll let you know how it turns out." I gave her a brief kiss, found the handwritten recipe, snapped a picture of the recipe with my cell phone, and flew out the door.

Our Burger Barn was a little different than others because they sell breakfast, lunch, and dinner. We're such a small town, that this was pretty much the only thing open for breakfast besides the sub shot and the two cafés. And where there's breakfast, there's old men hanging out, drinking coffee, ready to swap gossip and stories just like ladies do.

I went to the counter, ordered my drink, then slid into the booth across from Paige. She didn't look too great this morning.

"So, what's up?" I asked.

"I'm just so upset."

"Yeah, but it's not like it's a surprise, right?"

"How can you say that? I mean, I guess you're right, but still…I don't know what I'm going to do," Paige all but wailed.

"Why do you have to do anything?" I asked. "It's not like it affects you."

Paige stared at me like I was an idiot. I watched her blow her hair out of her eyes. Paige's hair was cut right below her chin in short, choppy layers. It was deep auburn with caramel blonde highlights. Her eyes were green, her nose perky, and her lips full. Between her and Mindy, I always felt frumpy.

"Of course this affects me!" Paige sobbed.

Oh, God. She wasn't going to tell me she did it, was she? She actually went to that old bat's house, subdued her, and then grabbed vital organs? No, no. This is Paige. Sensible, sweet Paige. Stay calm.

"I'm sorry," Paige sniffed. "I'm just so upset about this."

"I understand. But it's not like we liked her, right?"

Paige stopped crying but continued to dab her eyes. Even with red swollen eyes she managed to look great. "What? I'm talking about the fact that your brother and I are getting ready to celebrate our one-year anniversary, and I don't think he's going to give me a ring!"

Relief soared through my body. I tried to be sympathetic, I really did. After all, I'd probably be a little mad if the boy I'd loved for nearly my whole life still hadn't proposed, but what the heck did I know?

"Hey," I said, hoping to cheer her up. "I have to go downtown to Legends to get quotes from people over what happened last night. Wanna go with me?"

Paige perked up at this. "Sure. I'll tell you, Ryli, I was shocked when Matt dropped by this morning and told me what happened. I just can't believe it. Was it really that bad?"

"Yes, it was really that bad."

CHAPTER 4

The first thing I noticed when Paige and I stepped inside the salon was that it looked like a zoo. Two toddlers about three years old were crawling on the floor, playing in the hair that had fallen on the ground. Their mothers were oblivious to this disgusting act because they were too busy yammering away at one another. Hands were being thrown in the air with excitement, hair dryers were blowing, and the gossip was being tossed around like a beach ball. The volume was deafening.

I wasn't quite sure where to start. Paige and I hadn't even been noticed when we walked in. I guess no one could hear the dinging of the bell over the cacophony of other sounds. Cindy Troyer was blow drying Anna Johnson's hair, while Patty Carter was regaling them with what she'd already heard about the murder.

Knowing Patty, she'd probably heard a lot already. Patty was a nurse out at the Granville hospital. She used to be a nurse at the school years ago until Dr. Garver suddenly fired her. There was definitely no love lost between those two.

The other stylist, Tina Anderson, was setting Claire Hickman's hair in rollers. My God, what had Claire done, walked straight over from her graveyard shift? Didn't these people have a life? Lined up against the wall, sitting patiently waiting and gossiping amongst themselves, were four other women.

I walked over to Iris's nail station. She was sitting on a black vinyl stool painting Janice Tillman's nails. You'd never know Iris was a successful businesswoman who owned a thriving salon. She always dressed from decades past. Today she had on a button-down jean shirt tucked into a pair of pleated, high-waisted, acid-washed jeans. Her hair was a dull brown, and she still curled her short hair every morning with a curling iron and then feathered it out on the sides.

Janice and Iris had a love-hate relationship. Their typical M.O. was to get into a catfight over something ridiculous, back stab each other publicly, then down a few bottles of wine and make up. They once went three weeks without speaking—it was the quietest the town had ever been!

I had to clear my throat twice before they even acknowledged me. When recognition hit, they both sat up straighter.

Leaning in my general direction, Iris asked, "Ryli, honey, are you here to write about *the murder*?"

I barely suppressed a grimace. "Yes. I was hoping to maybe get some quotes from a couple ladies on what they're feeling."

"Well," Janice interjected. "I always knew if someone was going to be killed, it would be that woman. There probably won't be a single tear shed for her at her funeral."

"I heard they weren't gonna have a funeral, they're gonna have a memorial service instead." This from Debbie Smith sitting against the wall.

"Really? I hadn't heard that." Janice said. "Although, I have to say, it will be weird not seeing her in the salon anymore."

Deep breath, Ryli. Deep breath.

I took out my pad and pen. "What I'm really looking for is reaction as far as personal safety. Maybe reaction on what it means for the town, the school."

Iris scowled. "What it means is that we've just started the new school year and now suddenly we're without a superintendent. Do you know how long it'll take to get another?"

"I know," Janice the minion chimed in. "This is *so* inconvenient."

I turned to the ladies sitting against the wall. "Could I get your reaction about what happened last night?" I asked.

"I heard it was pretty gruesome." I turned and saw Sister Sharon Williams, my preacher's wife, standing next to me. I have to say I was a little surprised to see her there, clutching her purse as though it was her lifeline. Today she was dressed in a brown A-line skirt, white blouse buttoned up to her neck, and brown orthopedic slip-on shoes. Probably why I didn't hear her come in and walk up behind me. "Were you there, Ryli?"

"Yes, I was."

"Was it really as bad as they've been saying?" Sister Williams' bluish lips whispered.

"Yes, was it?" Debbie asked. I saw the gleam of hope in her eye. The hope of hearing first-hand all the gory details that she could tell people.

There was no way around this. "Yes, it was brutal."

Sister Williams sighed. "But at least the good Lord gave her some time here on Earth. Iris, I stopped by hoping I could get an appointment today, but I see you're busy."

Iris didn't even bother looking up from Janice's nails. "Yep, sure am. Try back later, will ya?"

This time I heard the bell ding above the door, signaling another arrival. I glanced over and saw Garrett standing by the door. He motioned to me with the crook of his finger. My heart raced. I know I should play hard to get, but who am I kidding...I nearly ran to him.

"I saw Paige's car and thought maybe you two were together."

I smiled in response. Mainly because I was afraid I'd say something stupid.

"I was thinking," Garrett said. "Why don't I pick you up around six and we can drive over to your brother's for dinner tonight."

Be still my heart!

I went for casual. "Sure. But you know we don't have to be there until seven, right? It only takes five minutes to...oh, right." I trailed off lamely.

Garrett's eyes bore into mine and he smiled that predator-like smile.

* * *

Closing the heavy oak door of Legends behind me, I breathed a sigh of relief. I'm not sure when I'd heard more cackling women in all my life. I was just getting ready to open Paige's car door, praying for Calgon to come take me away, when I felt a hand on my arm.

"Hey, Doc," I said, surprised to see Dr. Martin Powell hanging out downtown on a Friday morning. Doc Powell was the local veterinarian and current president of the school board. He loved Miss Molly almost as much as I did. He always sneaks her extra cat treats on her visits.

He was attractive in that Sean Connery way. In fact, for about a year now I'd been trying to set Mom up with him. His wife, Pearl, had died some years back from breast cancer, and he'd never remarried. Being a handsome, single doctor guaranteed him a homemade dinner from a different woman each night. He accepted the food, but never the company from what I'd heard through the grapevine. Still, it didn't stop me from bringing up my mom every time I had an appointment with him.

"What brings you to town this morning?" I asked.

Doc's green eyes bore into mine. "I just finished talking with the ladies down at central office about Dr. Garver."

Central office was where the superintendent, her secretary, and a couple other school officials had their offices. I could tell by the look on his face it hadn't gone well.

"No one can believe this has happened," Dr. Powell said.

"Yeah," I agreed. "It was pretty shocking."

Dr. Powell peered down into my face. "How're you doing? I heard you were there and saw the body."

Man, I'll never get over how fast word travels in this town.

"Doing about as good as can be expected," I said.

Dr. Powell glanced over at Legends. "Did you just come from in there?"

I couldn't help but laugh at his expression. It was the exact same one I had when I came out a second ago.

"Hi Doc," Paige said, popping out from the driver's side.

"Hello, Paige. I was just telling Ryli here how saddened we are at the sudden loss of Dr. Garver."

I couldn't help but wonder if he really was…saddened by this news, I mean. I'd always heard the two doctors didn't get along very well. In fact, if rumors could be believed, the last board meeting had resulted in a doozy of a fight between the two of them.

"Paige and I were just questioning some of the ladies inside, hoping for a quote for the paper," I said, trying to fill the awkward silence.

Doc scowled and his lips became a flat line of disapproval. "Oh, I'm sure you got plenty from that group in there." Giving himself a little shake, Doc smiled again at us. "Ladies, you have a lovely day. And, Ryli, give Miss Molly an extra treat for me tonight, would you?"

"Sure thing, Doc."

Paige and I watched Dr. Powell make his way down the street, waving at people that called out to him. I wasn't quite sure what to make of the strange conversation we'd just had, other than to say trying to find something nice to say about Dr. Garver was an awkward experience for everyone.

Paige dropped me off at Burger Barn. I hopped in my car and drove over to the office. I knew Hank would be livid I didn't get more than I did, but I couldn't *make* people say what I wanted them to say. I parked and walked inside.

"Well, what did you get?" Hank demanded.

"Nothing. All I got was hounded about the crime scene."

Hank narrowed his eyes at me. "How was the crime scene? And don't give me some political bull about how you can't talk about it. I'm your boss. You tell me everything."

I barely refrained from rolling my eyes. "You know I'm not telling you anything I shouldn't. I'll have something in half an hour." I turned and walked toward Mindy, my safety net.

"Honey, you want some tea before you start? Might help you relax and think."

"Yes, thanks."

Now that I'd had a few more hours to really think about what had happened, it didn't take me long to plunk out a story about Vera Garver's death and throw in my one lame quote from the salon.

I came up for air around lunch. Mindy made us a sandwich with chips while I put the finishing touches on the story. I hit send on the e-mail as I finished my sandwich.

"I heard they weren't going to have a funeral but a memorial service instead," Mindy said as she munched on her chips.

"I heard the same thing this morning at the salon."

"Wonder why that is?" she asked.

"I don't know. Weird."

Hank came out of the room waving my submitted story. "It'll do."

At two-thirty I made the announcement I had to get going. Hank was pretty good about letting me make my own hours as long as I met my deadlines.

"What's going on?" Mindy asked.

I didn't know if I should tell her. After all, she's my friend, but she's also my boss's wife. What do I say? That I'm going home to shave my legs because I may or may not fool around tonight.

"I'm going to Matt's tonight for dinner," I said. "I wanted to stop by the store so I can bake a dessert."

Hank snorted. "One death this week isn't enough?"

"Bite me," I said.

Mindy laughed. "Hank! Be nice. So just the three of you?"

I stared at her. How does she do that? Like she knows I'm hiding something. "No. Garrett is picking me up. We're going together."

Mindy squealed. "You know what this means, right?"

"It means she's probably gonna go and get herself knocked up," Hank growled. "I'm not giving you better insurance." He shoved the unlit cigar into his mouth and stalked back to his office.

CHAPTER 5

I drove to the grocery store and picked up the ingredients Mom's recipe called for before driving home. I'd read over the recipe a few times, so I was pretty sure I had everything down pat. There were a few things I wasn't sure about, but I figured I could wing it. After all, it's a chocolate cake with whip cream filling wrapped up like a huge Ho Ho. How hard could it be? And, yes, I was purposely going for the subliminal message.

The air was crisp and smelled of rain as I gathered the groceries from my trunk and headed inside the house. I knew Matt was going crazy over the fact it was less than ten days until Halloween, and I hadn't even started to decorate the cottage. I shut the front door with my hip and greeted Miss Molly.

After putting the groceries away, I made a list of things I wanted to get done before I started on the dessert. Bubble bath, shave all necessary body parts, and then work on my hair and makeup. This way when I finished the dessert all that would be left would be to shimmy into my black skinny jeans and sweater. Seemed simple enough. The dessert should only take about an hour to prepare and bake.

I opened a bottle of pinot noir and carried my wine glass and cell phone into the bathroom. Pouring the vanilla-lavender scent into the running water, I sat on the edge of the claw-foot tub, lit some vanilla candles, and sipped on wine while the tub filled.

Opening the Pandora app on my phone, I chose the station I wanted and slipped into the warm water.

The ringing of my cell phone jolted me awake. I knew from the ringtone it was Paige. Wiping my hands on the hand towel beside the tub, I decided to put her on speaker so I didn't accidentally drop the phone in the water.

"So tell me again what you're bringing tonight?" That was Paige, straight to the point.

"It's a chocolate roll with a whip cream center. Kinda like a huge Ho Ho."

"Could you be more obvious, Ryli?" Paige laughed.

"I'm getting ready to go start it now," I said, ignoring her question. "I figure I have plenty of time, but just in case I need to improvise I'll start early."

"Um...will you be insulted if I make a little dessert too?" Paige quickly added, "You know, just in case? I promise not to bring it out if yours is good." I could tell by her voice she really wanted me to say it was okay.

"That's fine. I mean, you won't need to, but I understand." Not really, but what the heck. I'd let them eat their words soon enough.

I finished shaving and then stepped out of the tub. I slathered on my favorite body lotion and wrapped myself in a short, red bathrobe. The satin robe felt empowering as I tied off the belt. Smelling good, feeling sassy, this diva was ready to tackle the dessert.

Twenty minutes later I realized I may have been a little too optimistic. For the life of me I couldn't figure out what I was doing wrong. All you had to do was add egg whites and tartar and then beat until stiff peaks formed. Then you add all the ingredients together and bake.

Glancing at the clock I noticed I only had an hour before Garrett was due, and I had yet to fix my hair and get dressed. Running into my bedroom I turned on my curling iron and started pulling clothes from my closet, trying to find my red clingy sweater and black skinny jeans. By now I figured I'd need all the help I could get. If I couldn't knock his socks off with my baking, maybe I could knock them off with my sexiness.

Oh, boy...I'm in trouble!

Thirty minutes later my hair was curled, my black jeans were skintight, and my sweater was pushed up and clinging in just the right spots. I zipped up my knee-high black boots over my jeans and did a little twirl and shimmy in the mirror, just to make sure everything was in place.

Feeling more confident, I walked back into the kitchen ready to tame the cake. Tying an apron around my waist, I once again went back to the recipe. If I could get it mixed together real quick, I could slap it in the oven with plenty of time to bake. While it was baking I could whip up the filling. We didn't have to be at Matt's house until seven, so I was still making good progress.

Dumping everything into the garbage can, I started over. I separated more eggs and prayed the peaks would get stiff this time. I carefully measured out the tartar, dumped it into the metal bowl, and turned on the KitchenAid my mom bought me as a housewarming gift.

Please, let this work!

The doorbell rang and my heart dropped. I kept the mixer running in hopes the mixture would stiffen shortly. Carrying my glass with me—added security—I paused at the front door to alternately wipe off my clammy hands on the apron. Plastering a confident smile on my face, I opened the door.

You know those moments when you're pretty sure time has slowed down and yet things are continually going on around you at what seems like warp speed? That's what it was for me. Just the sight of him in dark jeans and a long-sleeved shirt had me salivating. The color of his shirt was almost a perfect match for his icy, blue eyes. I realized he was devouring me in the same way, and I suddenly wished I would've taken off my apron.

"You look sexy as all get out in that apron, Sin."

"I'm just finishing up the filling." Okay, little white lie, but who's keeping track.

He gave me a peck on the cheek then walked toward the kitchen.

"What the—" Garrett was peering into the mixing bowl, his brow furrowed.

"It just needs to set up a little," I assured him.

A wicked grin spread across his face as he stared at me. "I don't think so, Sin." He reached up to turn off the mixer.

"Hey, it's not quite done!"

"What are these green floaty things?" He looked over at my ingredients, and the emotions on his face ranging from horror to amusement back to horror made me feel ridiculous. I wasn't sure what I had missed, but it must have been a doozy.

"Sin, what's in this bowl?" Garrett asked.

"Egg whites and tartar."

"Please tell me you know there's a difference between tartar sauce and cream of tartar."

There is?

"Holy crap! You put tartar *sauce* in here? Oh, that's priceless!" He leaned over the counter, holding his side. I could see his shoulders shaking. I knew there was a problem, but I wasn't sure exactly what it was.

"What?" I said as I went to stand next to him. "Okay, I obviously know I messed up, but what exactly did I do wrong?"

He must have heard the hurt in my voice because he lifted his head then stood back up. "Oh, babe, you know tartar sauce is what you put on fish, not in desserts, right?"

I could feel my face burning. Of course there would be a difference, but I'd never heard of cream of tartar. Mom's recipe just said to add six egg whites to one-eighth teaspoon of tartar. There were no specifications about what *kind* of tartar.

I thought tartar was tartar.

Tears stung my eyes, and I tried to blink them back. I would not cry in front of Garrett, especially after he just finished laughing at me.

Reaching up, Garrett brushed his thumb over my cheek. "Hey, don't worry. We have plenty of time before we need to leave. We can whip something up." He looked at the ingredients I had sitting out. "Do you have vinegar?"

"Vinegar? Why?"

"Because I'm fairly certain you don't have buttermilk, but if you have vinegar I can make buttermilk. I make the best chocolate cake you've ever tasted, and it only takes thirty-five minutes to bake. By the time we assemble and bake, we should be right at an hour. We'll still be on time, and no one will be the wiser."

I was stunned. I couldn't believe he was going to do this for me. "Do you need a recipe?"

"Nope. I make this one all the time. Trust me."

Kimble bakes…who knew?

The only other person that would know I didn't bring what I had originally intended to bring would be Paige, and she wouldn't say anything. Now, if Matt knew, I'd never live it down.

Grinning, I leaned over and kissed him lightly on the lips, "Deal!"

"We do have a few minutes to spare if—" I ducked under his arms as he tried to pull me closer.

"We don't have much time," I said. "We can hanky-panky later."

Garrett laughed as he poured the tartar sauce goop down the drain. "Hanky-panky? Really, Sin, who says that?"

Because he was helping me, I let the nickname slide.

We worked silently for a few minutes, Garrett assembling the ingredients while I cleaned up after him. "What were you trying to make?"

I bit my lip. I knew if I said a giant Ho Ho he would just poke fun at me. Especially since it didn't work. I fumbled around, unsure of how to answer.

"I don't know. Like a chocolate roll or something," I mumbled.

Garrett stopped pouring the batter into the pan. The twinkle in his eye told me I was caught. "A chocolate roll? You mean one of those cakes that looks like a giant Ho Ho?"

I refused to answer. Instead I brushed invisible crumbs off the counter.

"This has about thirty minutes to bake. Then it needs time to cool so I can dust some powdered sugar over the top." He leaned toward me and I sucked in my breath. I knew he was going to kiss me. The sudden ringing of his cell phone jarred me back into reality.

"Sorry, but I'm expecting a call back from the lab about evidence we bagged." Sliding his finger across the phone, he turned his back to me. "This is Kimble."

I'm not ashamed to say I openly eavesdropped. What else did I have to do? Unfortunately, Garrett was being tight lipped and only giving one-syllable answers followed by occasional grunts.

"What was that about?" I asked when he hung up.

"Nothing," Garrett replied as he reached for me again.

"Nothing? It didn't sound like nothing. Did the lab techs find something?"

Garrett narrowed his eyes at me. "Didn't I tell you yesterday to back off meddling in this case?"

"I'm not meddling. I'm just a concerned citizen."

"Don't push it, Sin. I have enough to worry about right now without worrying about your safety. I swear, I find out you're poking around where you don't belong, I'll haul you to jail."

I rolled my eyes. "Jeez, don't worry. I'm not going to do anything that will make your life crazy." I crossed my fingers behind my back.

Garrett snorted. "Right. I need to call Officer Ryan real quick. Can I use your bedroom for privacy?"

I waved my hand toward the hallway. "It's back there. I'm sure you can find it."

Garrett grinned and walked down the hallway. I sighed and sat down on the couch and waited for the cake to finish baking.

* * *

"Why are you here on time?" Paige whispered to me as I handed her the cake.

"What do you mean?" I honestly didn't catch on until she gave me the "knowing" look combined with the wiggling eyebrows.

"Whose car is that in the drive?" I said, hoping to distract her.

It worked. "Since there's no football game this week, Nick stopped by.

I really liked Nick Turner. He moved to Granville about two years ago when he took a teaching and coaching position at the high school.

"I wonder if he's heard anything new about the murder?" I whispered to Paige. I didn't want Garrett to hear me and give me another lecture.

I helped Paige prepare the salad, neither one of us talking much since the guys were within earshot.

"We're going to put the steaks on," Matt said as he led the guys outside.

"Okay, dish," Paige said once we were alone.

"Not much to tell. He came over, and we baked a cake."

"He came an hour early, and you're telling me you guys only baked a cake?"

"Yep."

Clucking her tongue in sympathy, Paige took a closer look at the cake. "What happened to the Ho Ho thing?"

"Didn't work out."

Paige being the good friend she was didn't say a word.

Dinner was a delicious meal of salad, grilled veggies, steaks, and the chocolate cake I brought.

"So, anything new you can share with us about Dr. Garver?" Matt asked suddenly.

Every eye turned to Garrett. "Not really. Looking into a few leads, but still going through the preliminaries right now."

There were leads? When did this happen? I wished I'd taken more care to listen to the phone call Garrett received at my house a while ago, since now suddenly there were leads.

"Everyone at the school is shocked," Nick said. "I heard the heart was ripped out of her chest."

Oh boy! Obviously word had gotten out already about Dr. Garver's body. Not that I really thought it would be able to be kept a secret in this town.

* * *

The ride back to my house after dinner was silent and semi-comfortable. I kept stealing sideways glances at Garrett, trying to read his face, but he was like granite. I bet he was awesome at poker.

As he pulled into my driveway, I unbuckled my seatbelt. He put the car in park, and I countered back by reaching for the door handle.

"Let me walk you to the door."

A command, not a request.

We both got out and walked up the porch steps and stopped at my front door. "Keys." He held out his hand. I reached into my jeans and pulled out my keys. In one fluid motion Garrett had the key inside the lock and the door open.

I cleared my throat. "Well, I guess—"

I never got a chance to finish. Garrett leaned down and kissed me. Before the panic of what to do next settled over me, Garrett broke off the kiss. "So, I think I'm going to say good night here. I've a long day tomorrow. Need to start working on those leads."

Never one to curb my tongue I asked, "What leads exactly?"

Garrett just chuckled. "Nope. Not gonna happen, Sin"

Pouting, I narrowed my eyes at him. "I know these people. What makes you think you can get somewhere with them that I can't?"

His eyes went hard. "Because it's my job, and I know how to do my job. Unlike you, I've had training in how to read people, look for tells when they're lying, follow clues, and solve crimes."

I rolled my eyes. I couldn't help it. Stupid to grab the bull by the horns, but sometimes I can't help myself. "I still have to do some writing and interviewing for the paper, especially now that people seem to know a little about what happened to the body." Knowing I was playing with fire, I couldn't help adding, "I'll tell ya what…if I come across anything important in my *journalistic* investigation, I'll let you know."

With that I walked into my house and shut the door. I swear I heard growling on the other side of the door but I chose to ignore it, because suddenly I had an epiphany as to who could help me with my investigation. It wasn't something I wanted to do, but if anyone could help me profile and hunt for clues, it was my great-Aunt Shirley.

CHAPTER 6

Saturday mornings are busy at Legends. I knew if I wanted to prove to Garrett that I could get answers, Legends was the first place I needed to stop.

The spaces in front of Legends were filled, so I drove around the corner and parked down the back alley. Usually cars didn't park here, unless you were like Iris and lived above the store. I saw Iris's car parked next to a big green dumpster. The only other spot to park was on the other side of the trash receptacle, sandwiched between the brick building and the dumpster. It was perfect. My car would be hidden out of sight.

As I made my way around the back of the deserted brick building, I wasn't watching where I was going and stumbled.

"Be careful there, dear. You don't want to get yourself hurt."

I glanced up quickly. Sister Sharon Williams was carrying a Steve's Sub Shop bag and gliding toward me. Her kind smile immediately put me at ease and my heart stopped pounding.

"Are you okay, Ryli?" Sister Williams held out her arm as if to steady me.

"Yeah. I was just thinking about the story I needed to get and wasn't paying attention." I glanced down at her bag and stated the obvious. "You and the preacher having breakfast out this morning?"

"Pastor loves his Steve's Sub Shop breakfast. It's a Saturday tradition of ours." She wiggled the plastic bag as she stepped around me.

Inspiration hit me. "Sister Williams, I was wondering if you would like to talk about Dr. Garver's death. I know y'all were friends, and that she was even on the church board."

The smile left Sister Williams's face. I felt awkward as I waited for her reply. "My dear, this is a very difficult time for us all. I'm not sure I can help you out." Her tone was polite, yet final.

I tried again, "I know, but sometimes talking about it helps." Okay, even to me it sounded lame, but it was worth a shot.

Once again she was quiet as she looked me over. "I cannot tell you how to do your job, Ryli, and I'm sure you don't mean to be disrespectful, but please remember that people grieve in different ways. I do not wish to talk about her death at this time. I'd like to grieve privately, if you don't mind."

Now I was officially embarrassed.

"It's not like that," I assured her. "I'm really trying to help out. Maybe even get some leads for Chief Kimble by asking questions."

Now where did that come from?

A placating smile formed on Sister Williams's face. "I'm sure the Chief can do his job just fine. Besides, I doubt the killer will be happy if you poke around and start asking questions. You be careful now, okay." She patted me on the arm and continued walking to her car. I stood there and watched as she drove off.

Did she mean be careful and watch where I was walking so I didn't stumble again, or be careful whom I asked questions to because she's afraid I'd end up like Dr. Garver?

A sobering thought.

My enthusiasm had severely dampened by the time I reached the front door of Legends and stepped inside. My senses were immediately assaulted with the smell of perm solution and hairspray. A chair was open along the wall of ladies waiting their turn, so I decided to take a seat and listen in.

"I know Coach Starns was irate about what she did with his budget," Pamela Nettles said.

Dan Starns has been the athletic director at the school for about five years now. He was a family man, two kids, nice wife. Somehow I couldn't see him committing such a heinous crime, but I decided to jot down his name anyway and stop by and talk with him. See if I couldn't pick up on something.

"Ryli, I didn't see you slip in. Did you need something in particular today?" Iris asked as she continued to tease Mrs. Evans's hair into a football-like bouffant.

"Just working on my editorial for the week." I tried to be nonchalant, but I knew if there was anything new and juicy, Iris would know about it by now. "Have you heard anything more about the Garver murder?"

Iris paused mid tease and looked me over from top to bottom, as though assessing my worth.

"I'll tell ya what, the shop's closed Monday, but I need to run a few errands during the day. Why don't you drop by my place Monday night? I might be able to help you out."

I couldn't believe my luck! Oh, I was so going to make Garrett eat his words!

Playing it cool I said, "Sure, Iris, that'd be great. I'll see you around seven o'clock Monday night," I said.

"Sounds good. Just come upstairs."

I drove out to Paige's place to see if she wanted to go with me to visit Dan Starns. I wasn't really sure what I was going to say to him or even what questions to ask, but I figured if he was hiding something, Paige and I would be able to see something.

Paige was finishing up a ledger for her dad, so I decided to put some tea on the stove. I wasn't sure yet how I was going to break it to her that we may need to bring Aunt Shirley into the mix. Paige and Aunt Shirley didn't exactly see eye to eye. Mainly because a while back Aunt Shirley told Paige the reason Matt still hadn't proposed was because a guy doesn't buy the cow when the milk is free. This did not go over well with Paige.

Paige strolled into the kitchen as I finished pouring our tea. "When Garrett dropped me off last night, he basically said we needed to butt out and stop asking questions because we wouldn't know a lead or a clue if it bit us on the butt." I was paraphrasing a little, but I needed her to agree to bring in Aunt Shirley.

"That's a little harsh, even for Garrett," Paige said as she blew on the tea.

"But it got me to thinking. Maybe he's right, maybe we need to bring in someone who *would* recognize a clue or a lead." I glanced at her to gauge her reaction when she finally figured out what I was saying.

"Oh no!" she exclaimed. "No way am I working with that crazy old woman!"

"Please, Paige! It's the only thing I can think of. I thought we might go visit her after we talk to Coach Starns. Who knows, maybe he'll give us something and we won't need her." I left her with that little glimmer of false hope.

I knew where Coach Starns lived because it used to be my old piano teacher's house when I was a kid. In fact, it was still referred to as her house by many, even though the Starns family had lived there for about three years now. Typical behavior in a small town.

I pulled into the driveway in front of the two-car garage. One garage door was open, so I figured someone must be home. I have to be honest, I wasn't even sure what I was going to say yet. I knew I couldn't come right out and ask him if he murdered Dr. Garver, but there had to be something or someone he could steer me toward. Turning off the car, Paige and I made a beeline for the garage.

A sandy-haired boy of about eleven ran around the corner of the house, skidding to a halt in front of the open garage. He didn't even look in our direction.

"Dad, can I go to Blake's to play?"

"Your chores are done?" a voice called from inside the garage.

"Yep," the boy said, hopping up and down in excitement. "Mom said it was fine but I had to ask you."

"Take your bike."

Running over to a rack of bikes, the boy yanked one free and hopped on. Hunching over the handlebars, he barely glanced at us as he flew by. I lifted my hand to wave, but he was already gone.

"Can I help you?"

I turned back toward the garage. Coach Starns was wiping his hands on a towel as he walked toward us. I knew he recognized me because I often go to games and athletic banquets to take pictures for the paper. He'd always been a nice enough guy, but suddenly I was glad I wasn't alone. I had to start toughening up if I was going to investigate this murder.

"I was hoping you can answer some questions for me about Dr. Garver's death."

"Look, I'll make it simple for you. I didn't kill her, and I don't know who did. I have a huge list of people who hated her, but I'm sure you also have one yourself."

He had me there.

"I guess I was hoping you might know something that could help us out. I didn't figure you killed her," I said, hoping to get him to open up, "but anything you know would be helpful."

Coach Starns chuckled. "Look lady, Chief Kimble already called me this morning. He said he'd be over sometime this afternoon to talk with me. He also told me if a certain nosey reporter came snooping around, I was to tell her nothing or I would be brought up on obstruction charges. And then he'd throw you in jail for the same thing."

I heard Paige gasp.

"Well, then I guess there's no reason to tell him I was ever here, right?" I said.

Coach Starns grinned. "Right, you were never here."

Paige and I ran to my car. I slid over the hood *Dukes of Hazzard* style, jumped in, and sped off down the street before Garrett caught us and hauled us off to jail.

* * *

There're no words to describe my great-Aunt Shirley...except nutty, mean, smart, crazy, and old. Well, what do you know? I actually could describe her.

She currently resides at the Oak Grove Manor, a sort of assisted living facility for the elderly. She's my mom's aunt. My great-Aunt Shirley never had a thought she didn't express, which put most people on edge. Deep down, I really liked her and her eccentric ways. I think she's around seventy-five, but I'm not sure, and I've never been brave enough to ask.

Aunt Shirley was a true old maid. She never married nor had children. Instead, she bucked the system in a time period when women just didn't do that. To her parents' horror, she ran off to Los Angeles, California at the age of twenty-three and became a private investigator. Yep, you heard right. My great-Aunt Shirley was a real-life *Charlie's Angels* type of woman. Before *Charlie's Angels* was even a thing.

"I still can't believe we're doing this," Paige whined. "She's a complete whack job! What on earth could she tell us that we don't already know?"

I shrugged. "I don't know, but I'm telling you the woman is amazing when it comes to knowing and digging up things."

Turning onto Cherry Street, I made my way slowly to Oak Grove Manor, practicing what I'd say to get Aunt Shirley hooked into helping us. I didn't figure it'd be too tough, it's not like she had a lot to do.

Oak Grove Manor was an old, three-story brick building with patches of ivy clinging to the exterior. The outside looked pretty neglected and run down, a metaphor I'm sure for the old people housed inside the building. A few of the apartments had tiny balconies that looked like one person could squeeze onto them.

Paige and I walked into the massive lobby and bypassed the information desk. We went through the first set of doors to the right of the foyer and headed to the elevator.

Aunt Shirley lived in apartment number 366. As I knocked on the door, I wondered how hard it would be to turn the three into a six. I always wondered that same thing every time I stopped by.

"Quit pounding and come in!" Aunt Shirley's voice boomed from inside.

I turned the doorknob and went in, leaving Paige to shut the door behind her. It was a tiny apartment with the main living room/kitchen/breakfast nook all in one room, and a bedroom and bathroom down a narrow hallway off to the left. The one bonus about the tiny living space was that it did have a sliding glass door in the living room that led to one of the barely-there balconies.

The walls were white and bare. When she first moved in, Aunt Shirley refused to decorate the place, claiming she wasn't going to be there for more than a few months, so why waste the energy. A little over a year later she still believed that ridiculous fairy tale. But after her last escapade, I was fairly certain Garrett and Mom were never going to let her out.

Garrett had only been in town and on the job for a few weeks when he first met Aunt Shirley. I'd been at the newspaper office for fifteen minutes when he called me in a fit of rage. He had Aunt Shirley locked up in a holding cell and wanted me to come get her before he did everyone a favor and tossed the key. I could hear my aunt in the background yelling and cursing.

When I entered the station, three officers were hanging around smirking but refusing to make eye contact. I knew most of them…if they weren't saying anything, I knew it must be bad.

Rounding the corner into the holding cell area I stopped short. There was my Aunt Shirley with her white hair covered in leaves and black soot smeared on her face. Her clothes looked like they'd gone ten rounds with Miss Molly's claws and lost. Or I should say her shirt…she didn't seem to be wearing any pants.

I turned to glare at Garrett.

He looked even worse than Aunt Shirley. In fact, I had to bite my tongue to keep from laughing. His shirt was untucked in some places, torn in others, his hair and pants were wet, and two deep scratches ran across his cheek.

"What happened?" I demanded.

"Your crazy aunt went and—"

"Don't listen to him," Aunt Shirley interrupted. "He doesn't know what he's saying."

Garrett turned and glared at her. "I have the right to lock you up for a long, long time lady! Don't push your luck!"

Aunt Shirley flipped him the bird.

I bit my tongue even harder.

Throwing up his hands, Garrett stalked over to me. "I get a call from the local hardware store reporting that an old lady had just backed a '65 Falcon into their sign and never bothered to stop."

Aunt Shirley gasped. "First off, watch who you're calling old. And another thing, you can't *prove* it was me!"

"Wait! Tell me the Falcon is okay!" I demanded, scared to death my dream car was totaled.

"Ha! Darn straight it's okay," Aunt Shirley said from the jail cell bench. "Nothing can hurt that car."

Garrett let out a growl. "Not only are you the only person in town who owns a '65 Falcon, but they also have surveillance cameras on the front of their store. So I know for a *fact* it was you."

"Humph," Aunt Shirley said, crossing her legs. Not a good idea. I saw more thigh on her than I ever wanted to see.

"Ask her where her pants are," Garrett demanded when he noticed my visible shudder.

"Here's the thing," Aunt Shirley said. "I was on my way to the hardware store to pick up a new rake. I was getting out of the car when I noticed I accidentally forgot to put on my pants."

Come again?

"Wait," I said. "Hadn't you just been outside?"

"Now wait a minute!" Aunt Shirley stood up, her shirt riding even higher on her thighs.

"Sit down!" Garrett and I shouted.

Aunt Shirley plopped back down on the bench. "Anyway, like I said, I realized I accidentally forgot my pants and hightailed it outta there. I might have hit the sign. I'm not sure. So I go home to rectify the oversight." She crossed her arms over her sagging breasts and glared at Garrett. "I'm walking toward the house when I smell the fire—"

"Omigod!" I exclaimed. "There was a fire?"

"Oh, yes," Garrett said staring my aunt down.

Aunt Shirley held up her hand. "I'm telling the story. So anyway, I smell the fire and head to the back of the house. See, I'd raked a couple leaves and broken the rake, which was why I

60

needed a new one. Thing is, I *thought* I'd put out the fire before leaving to go to the store, but I guess not."

Garrett's jaw had a visible tic. "First, the fact we're under a no burn order should have been the first indication you shouldn't be doing this. Secondly, the fact you were outside raking pretend leaves *naked* should also be—"

"Pipe down," Aunt Shirley said. "I wasn't exactly naked."

I closed my eyes and counted to five. "Aunt Shirley, it's August. There are no leaves to rake."

"There were a few," Aunt Shirley countered.

"How did you all end up looking like you do?" I asked Aunt Shirley, not really sure I wanted to know.

"Well, when I noticed the leaves were on fire, I hurried and grabbed the hose. Suddenly out of nowhere this lunkhead," Aunt Shirley pointed to Garrett, "runs straight for me, screaming and yelling."

Garrett's scratched cheek had started to develop an alarming tic and his face was bright red. Knowing he was going to blow at any second, I fluttered my hands quickly for Aunt Shirley to continue. "So of course I got frightened! I'm just an old lady with a fragile heart condition." I knew this to be a lie. "My first reaction was to protect myself and my virtue, so I turned the hose on him."

"Even after I yelled for her to stop, she just kept on spraying me. Then a spark jumped onto her decrepit wooden shed and sent it up in flames."

"Hey," Aunt Shirley said, "watch who you're calling decrepit there, Ace!"

I put my hand up to stop Garrett from charging into the holding cell and clobbering my aunt. I remember it clearly because it was the first time I'd ever touched him.

It left an impression.

Aunt Shirley leaned forward on the bench. "As I turned to put out the fire on the shed, this baboon charges me, knocks me to the ground, and starts rolling around with me. Little pervert! Probably trying to get his jollies off on my account. What's the matter, boy, can't find a girl your own age?"

I laughed. I couldn't help it. The thought of big, hunky Garrett Kimble rolling around on the ground with my half-naked aunt was something I'd have paid to see.

"And just my luck," Garrett said, clenching his teeth, "my police backup and the fire station all showed up at this time to witness me on the ground with your aunt!"

I laughed even harder.

"I'm glad you see the humor in this," Garrett said dryly. "However, because of your aunt, I'm now the laughingstock of this community. Not the impression I wanted to give my first few weeks here."

"I'm sorry. I really am," I lied. "Did Matt see?"

"That whippersnapper nephew of mine had the *nerve* to lecture *me* about the dangers of fire and smoke inhalation. He's lucky I didn't knock him over the head with the oxygen tank he'd just given me," Aunt Shirley said. "I needed it at the time, mind you. Otherwise I would have. The youth today are so disrespectful to their elders!"

Garrett turned to me and unlocked the cell. "Get...her...out...of...here," he said slowly, "before I change my mind and throw the book at her."

Not needing to be told twice, I yanked open the cell and grabbed Aunt Shirley by the arm, shushing her when she tried to protest. I knew when enough was enough.

The whole episode resulted in my Aunt Shirley being placed at Oak Grove Manor, with the understanding that it would be permanent. Everyone understood that but my aunt.

So like I said, here we are a little over a year later, and my Aunt Shirley still believes she's here temporarily.

CHAPTER 7

Today Aunt Shirley was sitting on her couch, feet propped up, staring at a muted television. She was dressed in lavender polyester pants and an oversized blouse with huge flowers in every color splattered all over. I was glad to see she'd remembered her pants.

She was still pretty fit for a woman in her seventies. She had short, white hair that barely reached her ears, and her face sprouted more wrinkles than a shar-pei puppy. Although she was always quick to tell us about all the movie stars she dated in Los Angeles when she was in her prime.

"Well, well, if it isn't Janine's girl," Aunt Shirley rasped. "It's been so long I hardly recognized you."

I'd just been to see the old bat two weeks ago, but since I needed her help I let it go.

Aunt Shirley turned to Paige. "Hello, Paige. I haven't gotten a wedding invitation yet, so I'm assuming my great-nephew is still just enjoying all that free milk, eh?" Aunt Shirley hit her leg and exploded into laughter. Which resulted in a coughing fit. I started to worry when her face turned red and she started wheezing and coughing.

Time to get down to business before Paige killed her and we had yet *another* murder on our hands.

"Hey, Aunt Shirley, I was wondering if I could ask you some questions about things that've been happening around town." I tried to be vague so she wouldn't ask too many questions.

Aunt Shirley pulled open the drawer on the end table beside the couch and pulled out an electronic cigarette.

"Whaddaya wanna know?" Aunt Shirley asked as she inhaled on the contraption.

I was momentarily dumbfounded.

"Um, Aunt Shirley, you don't smoke."

"I know. And I never will now that I have this wonderful invention."

I tried again. "Is that one of those e-cigs?" I asked.

"Yep. I saw an ad on the Internet, said it was healthier than smoking cigarettes."

Sometimes if you say things slower and louder, people suddenly understand. Okay, I know that's a lie, but I'm always doing it. "Why do you think you need it? You don't smoke."

"I don't smoke *now*, but you never know, I may start taking up the habit someday. This little baby," she continued, shaking it around, "takes that worry away. It's sort of a sneak attack for preventative measures."

"I'm pretty sure there's no such thing," I said.

"You calling me a liar?" Aunt Shirley asked while sucking on the e-cig. The vapor suddenly shot out of her mouth and she started hacking and coughing. I could see tears forming in her eyes. I rushed over, ready to pound on her back, but she waved me off. "I'm okay," she wheezed, trying to take deep breaths.

"Doesn't that hurt your throat?" Paige asked, shaking her head at my aunt's ridiculous behavior.

"Only in the mornings. By mid-afternoon it subsides."

I closed my eyes and started counting to ten. I only made it to three before I blurted, "Maybe that's your body's way of saying stop using it!"

"Nonsense," Aunt Shirley said.

"Is there nicotine in that?" I asked.

"No." Aunt Shirley inhaled and wheezed and sputtered again. "I don't smoke cigarettes and never will. It's a disgusting habit."

I decided not to push the issue and instead got to the reason we were there. "Aunt Shirley, there was a murder Thursday night, and I was thinking—"

"I'm aware Dr. Garver was murdered," Aunt Shirley interrupted.

"You are?" Paige asked.

"Of course! I can still eavesdrop on a good conversation, you know. There's not an orderly around here that can keep their mouth shut."

"Anyway," I continued, "Paige and I thought maybe we could help Chief Kimble figure out who the murderer is."

Aunt Shirley squinted at me. "Why?"

I couldn't tell her the truth, that I wanted to help solve this murder to prove to Garrett he wasn't the only one who could solve a crime. That would just sound petty. "Journalistic reasons?"

Aunt Shirley made an annoying buzzer sound. "Try again. I think this has something to do with Barney Fife and how you've been sniffing around him when you think no one's watching."

I glowered at her. She and I both knew he was the exact opposite of Barney Fife. I also knew if Garrett ever heard her, he'd definitely lock her up and throw away the key.

"It has nothing to do—"

"Save it, girlie." Aunt Shirley said, cutting me off and inhaling on her vapor again. I could tell she was trying not to cough because her face turned dangerously red. I figured it served her right.

"We probably should help that whelp out," Aunt Shirley said. "If his debacle with me is any indication of how he runs things, he probably couldn't solve a murder if it was handed to him on a silver platter!"

Once again I held my tongue.

"Well, what do you got so far?" Aunt Shirley wheezed.

"We were thinking it was someone connected with—"

"I don't want to know *who*," Aunt Shirley said. "I want to know what the crime scene looked like. All of it. Don't leave anything out."

Okay, now I was a little worried. I knew I wasn't supposed to reveal anything about the scene, even though some people already knew some of the facts. There were still only a handful of people who knew the entire truth. If I said something now, I knew I'd be risking my job with the police department.

"Ain't nothing you say gonna leave this room, is it?" Aunt Shirley gave Paige a hard look.

"You don't have to worry about me," Paige said as she put her hands up in the air. "I'm now an accessory in this mess."

Chewing on my lip, I made a snap decision. "Okay, here's what really went down." I proceeded to tell them about the crime scene, about Dr. Garver's heart being removed and her fingertips being cut off. I didn't leave a single gross description out.

"Okay, now I'm hungry," Aunt Shirley said when I'd finished.

Paige whipped her head around to look at me. "Is she serious?"

"I never joke about food." Aunt Shirley said. "It's getting late. How about you take me to your house, Ryli, and make your dear great aunt some pancakes for lunch."

I crossed my arms over my chest. "Um...no. Besides, pancakes are for breakfast, not lunch."

"That's why you'll never solve this case alone," Aunt Shirley said. "You don't know how to think outside the box."

I sighed. "Fine. Wait here and I'll bring the car around and pick you up in front of the doors." I ignored the glare from Paige as I left her alone with Aunt Shirley.

A few minutes later I saw Aunt Shirley breeze through the front door of the retirement center. I heard her bellow before I even had her side of the door open.

"What in tarnation is this?" Aunt Shirley asked, crunching her nose up like she smelled something rotten.

"My car," I said.

Aunt Shirley snickered. "I ain't riding in this piece of crap car. I've got a real car we can drive."

Aunt Shirley's "real" car was the very car I'd coveted pretty much my entire life...a turquoise 1965 Ford Falcon that had a glass-like finish. Dancing across the hood and side panels were purple ghost flames. In fact, the flames were so deep that a person had to look hard to see them. Under the hood was a stock 302 with an Edelbrock fuel injection.

The interior was just as sweet. The barely-there dashboard was done in the same turquoise color, and the bucket seats in the front and bench seat in the back were a pristine white with turquoise stitching.

I knew Aunt Shirley had to garage the car after her hardware sign accident and the plethora of parking tickets she'd received prior...and it nearly killed her. The retirement center had a parking lot in the back where tenants could park one car for free. It just so happened that Aunt Shirley's balcony overlooked the parking lot, so she could keep an eye on her baby.

"Park this heap back where it was," Aunt Shirley said, "and let's do this in style. The Falcon always helped me clear my mind when I was on a case."

I didn't need to be told twice. I parked my old car and ran over to where Aunt Shirley and Paige were standing. Aunt Shirley dangled the keys in front of me.

"I never leave home without 'em. Let's go pull the tarp off her and see how she drives."

Hating the fact I had to be the adult here I asked, "Aunt Shirley, are the tags current?"

"You bet your sweet bottom they are. Now, let's ride!"

* * *

The drive from Oak Grove Manor to my house was exhilarating...but it was also torture.

"You wanna know who had it bad for me?" Aunt Shirley asked. "That Richard Burton. I gave Elizabeth Taylor a run for her money, ya know."

I rolled my eyes. Not for one minute did I believe a word of that story. I glanced in the rear-view mirror and saw Paige mouth the word "crazy" to me.

As I pulled the Falcon into my driveway, I noticed a package sitting on the porch. I didn't remember ordering anything off the computer, but I'm usually forgetful.

Stooping over to pick up the package, I let the girls into the house. Usually the UPS guy didn't come until after two. Must be my lucky day!

"I'll start breakfast while you guys put a list together," I said.

Aunt Shirley snorted. "You think that's a good idea? I figured Paige here would make the pancakes. Or is she like you and can't cook?"

"I can cook!" Paige and I shouted together.

Aunt Shirley just laughed. "Y'all are just too gullible."

Muttering and cursing to myself about not keeping arsenic on hand, I got out the necessary ingredients for pancakes. I decided to spice things up a bit and grabbed a bottle of cinnamon from my cabinet of spices. I'd show her who couldn't cook.

"So what do you two civilians have so far?" Aunt Shirley grunted as she hoisted her pink patent-leather purse onto my dining room table. I figured it had to weigh ten pounds easy.

"Aunt Shirley," I said, "you're a civilian, too. You were never in the military."

Shirley narrowed her eyes at me. "You don't know all the things I've done in my life. The private investigating gig was just the tip of the iceberg."

I rolled my eyes.

"Well," Paige said, hoping to stop another ridiculous fight, "we already made a list of the possible suspects."

I listened half-heartedly as they discussed the case, focusing mostly on flipping and preparing pancakes. When I had a plate full of piping hot cakes, I carried them and some maple syrup to the table.

"Here's where you're going wrong," Aunt Shirley said. "It's not someone associated with the school."

"How can you be so sure?" Paige asked.

"What major event has just taken place at the school?" Aunt Shirley asked as she took three pancakes from the plate.

"Nothing I can think of," I said as I went to get milk from the fridge.

"Exactly my point. One of the first things you do when profiling a murderer is ask yourself what's the stressor. Something big has had to happen to make the murderer want to start murdering."

Hmmm…that sounded good. Maybe Aunt Shirley was going to be handy after all.

"Also, now is not the time to kill someone so influential just for sport. This murder has crippled the school district. No one that works for the district would do something so drastic to the whole community. If they were going to kill her, they'd do it at the end of school. Gives everyone time to find a replacement."

Disturbing to think about…but I got her meaning.

"And why the fingertips?" Aunt Shirley continued. "It's saying more than just she didn't have a heart. It's more personal."

I watched her smother her pancakes in butter and maple syrup, spreading it evenly over the top. She cut a huge chunk off with her fork and stuffed it in her mouth.

Miss Molly wondered into the living room, winding her body slowly through my legs, meowing loudly. I knew what that meant.

"Hold on, Miss Molly. I'll get your food in a second."

I picked up a knife from the table and started to open the cardboard box I'd received. There was no return address on the box, just my name. I reached in and moved the packing peanuts aside.

I lifted the square, glass container out of the box and shook off the last of the clinging peanuts. I heard the "tink tink" sound of the contents hitting against the glass, but it wasn't until I heard Paige scream and saw her bolt from her chair that I realized something was wrong.

As if in slow motion, I brought the container up so I could easily peer through it. When my mind finally caught up with my eyes, I let out a blood-curdling scream so loud it hurt my throat. I was staring at a heart and three fingertips with Cherries in the Snow nail polish on them. I quickly dropped the glass container on the table, which caused even more tinkling sounds to fill the air.

Miss Molly jumped onto the table and began batting at the glass, as if she were trying to catch a mouse. Every time she moved the container with her paw and it made a tinking sound, I heard myself scream even more.

"For the love, could you two sissies stop screaming?" Aunt Shirley demanded. "You're giving me a headache."

I looked over at Aunt Shirley calmly eating pancakes and felt myself starting to gag. How in the world could she be eating at a time like this? Didn't she know what was inside the container…and how weird was it that I knew the nail polish color? I mean it was my favorite color and all, but *gross!*

By this time Miss Molly had ceased to be entertained by the glass and had taken up washing herself on the table. Out of habit I batted her off the table and then sat back down in a chair.

Paige stumbled back over and righted her overturned chair. Plopping down hard, she asked the question I'd been wondering, "Why would someone do this to you?"

"I'm not sure," I said. "Maybe because—"

"Maybe because you pissed someone off, duh," Aunt Shirley said as she waved her empty fork at me.

I didn't say anything…mainly because I was afraid she was right. Who had I angered enough to send me their little trophies as a warning?

Gag!

"Why did it make that weird sound?" Paige asked.

"I think they're frozen," Aunt Shirley said as she continued shoving pancakes into her mouth. "Killer must have put the heart and fingers in a deep freeze or something."

I have to admit, I kind of felt bad for Dr. Garver. It's one thing to be murdered, but to have your body frozen on top of it was actually quite sad.

"What should we do now?" Paige asked.

I knew what we had to do, I just didn't want to do it because Garrett was gonna be livid. Somehow this was going to be my fault.

"I'll tell you what you should do now," Aunt Shirley said as she pushed her half-eaten plate aside. "You should learn to make pancakes. These things taste like cow poop."

I narrowed my eyes at her. I'd just gotten some killer's trophies in the mail and she had the nerve to gripe about my pancakes! "What's the matter, Auntie? Is the cinnamon a little too much for you to handle in your old age?"

Aunt Shirley snorted. "Watch your mouth before I wash it out with soap. And believe me, that ain't no cinnamon."

More because I wanted to get away from the table than anything, I raced to the counter and grabbed the spice, shoving it in her face. "See, cinnamon."

Aunt Shirley started laughing. "Only thing I see is a bottle of cumin, you nitwit!"

I turned the label toward me and groaned. She was right.

"Truth be told, I think I'd rather eat that heart right there than another bite of your cooking," Aunt Shirley hooted.

Paige made a gagging noise.

Aunt Shirley ignored her. "You know who could cook? Sean Connery. He once made me breakfast. You catching' my drift here girls...breakfast!" Aunt Shirley said, wiggling her over-grown bushy eyebrows in a lewd, suggestive way.

Now I really did gag.

CHAPTER 8

"What the hell do you mean you don't know why the box came to you?" Garrett shouted.

We decided we had to call Garrett. There was no way around it. We also decided we'd keep the answers simple and not volunteer too much information. We didn't want to tip our hand, even though there was nothing to really tip just yet.

He arrived with another police officer in tow, and the two began collecting the evidence. I was just thankful it wasn't Officer Chunsey with him. Just like I knew would happen, Garrett was currently pacing in my living room, muttering to himself because I couldn't answer his questions.

I tried again. "Like I said, I don't know. I left kinda early this morning. I went and got Paige and we went a few places to ask some questions for the paper. Later, Paige and I went to visit Aunt Shirley, and we decided to bring her back to my house for pancakes."

"Keep talking," Garrett said.

I decided to take the higher ground and ignore his rude behavior. "I put the box on the table and started to make pancakes."

"She started to make some pancakes that tasted like horse manure she means," Aunt Shirley said from the lounging position of my recliner.

I glared at Aunt Shirley. "While Aunt Shirley was eating, I opened the box."

"Didn't you find it odd the box only had your name on it? It didn't have a return address, yet you decided to open it anyway." I could hear the sarcasm in his voice, but I chose to ignore it.

"I thought maybe I had ordered something off of the Internet and forgot. I didn't realize what was going on until Paige started screaming."

"You poor girl," Matt said to Paige as he hugged her against his body. "I still can't believe this happened to you."

Ummm...hello! I think it happened to me!

We decided to call Matt after we called Garrett, just in case we needed a cool head to prevail. When Matt heard that Paige was involved, he sped right over. I'm not quite sure how I felt about my brother being more concerned about the welfare of his girlfriend than the welfare of his own sister, but I'd deal with that little jealousy later. Basically he was just sitting next to Paige on the couch, stroking her hair, rubbing her hands, and making sympathetic cooing noises to her.

Meanwhile, I had Attila the Hun on me like an irate drill sergeant. Garrett never once asked me if I was okay, or held my hand, or stroked my hair.

Nope. He just automatically assumed I'd done something wrong. Which I probably did...but still, life was so not fair.

"Keep going," Garrett motioned to me.

"That's it. I opened the box and then we called you."

Garrett stopped pacing and looked at me. "So why you? What have you done recently to warrant this kind of action?"

"I don't know," I said. "And stop assuming I did something!"

Matt chuckled. I shot him my best evil eye. If he wasn't going to come to my rescue, then why was he even here?

"Okay," Garrett said, "so assuming the killer didn't always mean to drag you into this, then we can assume that it's someone you've been in contact with within the last seventy-two hours."

"That's like half the town!" I exclaimed. "I've questioned tons of people about the murder."

"Then we start with half the town. Make a list of people you have interacted with within the last seventy-two hours and give it to me ASAP," Garrett said. "Oh, and one more thing...why were you visiting your aunt? And please don't give me some ridiculous story about just wanting to see her. I know she used to be a private investigator. I'm going to assume it has *nothing* to do with dragging her into this mess you're in, right?"

I looked at Aunt Shirley. She gave me a tiny shake of her head. I remembered what she said about giving away as little info as possible. "Just a friendly visit is exactly what Paige and I were doing."

Garrett's tic suddenly became more noticeable. "Can you keep an eye on them?" he asked Matt. "I don't want anyone coming back to finish what they started."

"Sure," Matt said. "I'll take them all back to my place. There's more room there."

Aunt Shirley snorted. "I ain't going to your house, boy. I'm old enough to take care of myself. Been doing it for longer than you've been alive, and I'll keep doing it until the day I die. If ever a time comes that some man needs to hold my hand, then take me out back and shoot me!"

Garrett stared down my aunt with those steel, blue eyes.

She gave them right back.

Impressive.

"Suit yourself," Garrett relented.

"I always do!" Aunt Shirley replied.

I figured I'd drive the Falcon back to Oak Grove Manor and then drive my car over to Mom's house to stay the night. I wasn't excited about telling her what I'd gotten myself into, but I figured she couldn't be any madder at me than Garrett. Plus, I hated the idea of being a third wheel at Matt's house.

I was about to walk out the door when Garrett said, "Stay." He was leaning against my kitchen counter bar, looking like he wanted to be anywhere else.

"Or I could just drive the Falcon and Aunt Shirley back to Oak Grove Manor," I insisted. I actually didn't want to give the car up now that I'd had a taste of her.

"I noticed the Falcon was out and about," Garrett said, giving Aunt Shirley the eye.

"The girl can keep the car," Aunt Shirley growled.

My heart soared…had I heard right? I could keep the car!

Aunt Shirley turned to me. "Matt can take me home. You keep the car here, make it look like some badass chick lives here…not some sissy reporter."

At that moment I was so excited to have the car, I didn't care she'd just called me a sissy. The Falcon was mine!

I hugged Paige goodbye and promised I'd text her later to see how she was doing. "I got one of them cellular phones too, you know," Aunt Shirley pouted. "It sure would be nice if someone checked in on me...especially since I don't have a car anymore." The last part was said with a glare my way.

Message read loud and clear.

"I'll text you tonight too, Aunt Shirley," I said. "Make sure you're settled in fine."

"Well, don't go putting yourself out any. I'm sure I'll be just fine. I've dealt with worse when I was a private investigator."

Aunt Shirley...always the passive-aggressive one.

The front door closed and I turned to face Garrett. I didn't want to be alone with him in my house—especially when he was this annoyed with me. I avoided looking at him and started picking up the drinking glasses from the end tables.

"I'll just be a second," I said as I put the glasses in the sink. "I need to grab some clothes for church tomorrow and then we can go."

Garrett didn't say anything, so I sneaked a peek at him. He'd straightened from the bar and started walking toward me. I felt my pulse start to race and realized I was trapped in the tiny kitchen with him.

I braced myself for yelling, but instead he picked up one of my curls and started twirling it around his finger. For some reason, this panicked me even more. "Do you always attract danger, Sin?"

I laughed and relaxed a little. "No, trust me on this."

To my disappointment, Garrett let go of my curl. "Go get your clothes. I need to get back to the station."

I stuffed some clothes in a tote and left food in a dish for Miss Molly. I didn't want to take her to Mom's because I was afraid it would be too much for her. She was already in a tizzy that so many people had been traipsing through the house earlier.

The quick ride to Mom's house was in silence. I wanted to ask some questions, but I could tell by the stony look on his face he was done talking to me about the murder or the evidence he gathered from my house. He pulled into my mom's driveway and left the car running.

"I'll touch base with you either tonight or tomorrow after church," Garrett informed me.

I reached for the handle on the door. Before I could change my mind, I leaned over and gave him a quick kiss. "Be safe."

Garrett stared at me with those electric blue eyes, "Back at ya, Sin."

Then he winked at me. I fled from the car as fast as my feet could carry me.

* * *

Mom and I made it to church the next morning with ten minutes to spare. Mom stopped to talk with an elderly couple as I made my way to an open pew. I had just put my purse under the pew when I felt a tap on my shoulder.

"I'm just so shocked at what's happened," Sandy Trindle said as she slid closer to the front of her pew directly behind me. "I wonder when they'll hold an election to replace the position that's open now on the church board."

I shrugged. That was the last concern I had.

Sandy kept right on talking. "I overheard June Johnson tell Barbara Nelson during Sunday school that at the last church board meeting Dr. Garver and Pastor Williams got into a heated dispute over money."

Pastor Williams? Definitely worth looking into.

Just then Anna Johnson sat down next to Sandy. Anna, June's daughter, always looked so glamorous. I remembered her being at Legends the day after the murder. By the way her smooth tresses moved over her tan shoulders, her blow out was still holding up.

"Well," Anna said as she tucked a blonde strand behind her ear, "I heard Dr. Garver was gunning for a lot of people. She had Dan Starns jumping through so many hoops, I'm surprised he's stuck around this long. I bet he did a jig when he found out she was dead."

I was about to ask Anna to elaborate when the piano started, signaling the start of service. Mom and Paige both slid into the pew beside me, and I decided to file the rest of the questions away until a later time.

After church, we usually go out to eat. Today was no exception. Since there were only two restaurants in town open on Sundays, it wasn't a hard decision to make on where to eat. We decided on the Country Cafe. We were just about to be seated when Dr. Powell walked in alone. I knew it would be a perfect opportunity to see what he knew about the murder.

I sent him a wave. "Hey, Doc. Want to sit with us today?"

Dr. Powell looked slightly embarrassed but recovered nicely. "That would be lovely. That is, if you ladies don't mind the company."

My mom blushed. I knew she thought I was doing this as a hook up, but this time I just wanted to pick his brain. I sent her an innocent smile.

"We'd love it if you joined us," Mom said.

The four of us were led to a back corner booth—a perfect place for a little privacy. Mom and Doc both stopped many times on the way back to the booth to chat with people. Paige and I gave up waiting on them and went ahead and sat down.

"What's going on?" Paige asked. "Why did you invite Dr. Powell to join us?"

"I want to see if he knows anything more. I heard he and Dr. Garver were at odds over school board stuff. Maybe he'll give us some clues."

We didn't have long to wait before Mom and Doc joined us. Mom slid in next to me and Doc sat next to Paige.

"It's very nice of you all to invite me over," Doc said. "I usually just sit by myself most Sundays."

I gave mom a little nudge with my elbow. Obviously he was giving her a signal that he was single and available. She chose to ignore me.

The waitress came over and took our order. With the small talk out of the way, I decided to forge ahead.

"Doc, have you heard anything more about Dr. Garver's death?" I didn't say murder because I didn't want to put him off if he was in the mood to talk.

Doc Powell stirred his coffee but didn't say anything for a few seconds. "Not really, just what I've heard around town. Although, I did hear that there didn't appear to be a struggle, so my guess is whoever did this either has to be amazingly strong or was somehow able to subdue Dr. Garver."

Exactly what I thought.

Our meal came and we dug in. I didn't really pay much attention to what Mom and Doc talked about. I was more interested in the fact the suspect either had to be Arnold Schwarzenegger's body double, or someone who knew how to subdue someone. There had to be tons of ways to subdue someone, so that didn't get me too far ahead of where I currently was.

We bid farewell to Doc and headed back to Mom's. Paige and I went upstairs to call Aunt Shirley and see what our next move should be. I put her on speakerphone.

"Hey, Aunt Shirley."

"About dang time. Where've you been?"

I rolled my eyes at Paige. "Umm...church. It's Sunday after all." I added that last part as a dig for her skipping church.

She obviously didn't care. "I've been thinking," Aunt Shirley said as she took a deep breath and then started hacking.

"Put that thing away! You're seriously gonna hurt yourself!" I knew she was puffing away on that ridiculous e-cig.

"Anyway," Aunt Shirley said as though I hadn't spoken, "I know you said you were going to go see that loudmouth Iris on Monday. Maybe we should all go together. She did say she may have some information for you, didn't she?"

I chewed on my lower lip. I wasn't sure what to do. Did I really want Aunt Shirley and Paige with me when I talked with Iris about the murder?

Aunt Shirley must have sensed my hesitation. "Do you even know the questions you're gonna ask her?"

I sighed. She was probably right, I would need her help.

"I can come," Paige whispered.

"Fine," I said. "We'll come by to pick you up a little before seven tomorrow night."

"Dang right you will. I want to make sure my Falcon is doing okay."

An hour later, Matt's shift at the fire station finally ended. He pulled into the driveway and came inside to talk with Mom. By the time Mom stopped fussing over and feeding Matt, I was ready to pull my hair out. I love my mom, but I can only be away from my place for so long before I start climbing the walls.

After promising Mom I'd be careful and not do anything foolish, I hopped in Matt's truck. He took me to Oak Grove to retrieve my car. I drove it back to my house and parked it along the street in front of my house. My driveway was too small for two cars, and the Falcon was more important to me. Matt insisted on coming in and checking to make sure everything was safe before leaving.

A few minutes later, when I was finally alone, I sat down and started writing a list of the people I had interacted with on Friday and Saturday. There were all the ladies at Legends, Doc Powell, and Coach Starns. That was pretty much it. Did Garrett seriously believe that one of the ladies at Legends hacked up Dr. Garver?

There was no way. We obviously missed something. I was still pondering the list when my cell phone rang. My pulse raced when I saw the number.

"Hey Garrett," I said, trying to go for casual.

"Did you get me that list?"

Obviously he was going for formal and gruff.

"Yes. But I think you're on the wrong track. It was mostly old ladies from Legends." There was no way I was going to tell him I'd driven by Coach Starns's house. "We must have missed something. Maybe I was targeted because I'm writing a piece for the paper and asking questions. And when you put me up against Hank, I'm the easier target."

I could sense Garrett mulling that idea over. "Maybe. I just wish I knew for sure. How're you doing otherwise?"

"I'm doing okay. Matt dropped me back home, so I'm just piddling around."

"Well, I'm stuck here at the station for a bit. I need to finish going over a few things."

Darn. "Well, I have that list if you need it. But like I said, it's just the ladies from Legends."

"Please tell me you won't do anything crazy tomorrow."

Double darn. I hated the fact he assumed I'd do something rash, and I also hated the fact I was going to have to lie. There was no way I was going to tell him that the three of us were going to talk to Iris tomorrow night.

"Nope, nothing rash," I said as I crossed my fingers.

CHAPTER 9

What does one wear to interrogate a suspect?

I decided on black jeans, a black loose-fitting turtleneck, and my black boots. I was going for intimidating yet approachable. I knew I'd be lucky if Iris gave me anything useful. Still, a girl could hope.

I needed to catch a break. I'd spent the entire morning at the office researching ways a person could subdue another person, and the results were scary.

I picked Paige up at six-forty and we drove over to Oak Grove Manor to pick up Aunt Shirley. I wasn't sure what I was expecting when she opened the door, but I can definitely say it wasn't a long-sleeved black jumpsuit with Army boots and a camouflage bandana wrapped around her head.

"What's with the outfit?" I asked.

"I figured you two sissies would go for cutesy. I want Iris to know we mean business."

We all piled into the Falcon and headed over to Legends. Once again I parked in the back lot by the dumpster, out of sight of other cars driving by. We were about ten minutes early, but I didn't think Iris would mind.

I escorted the girls up the back wooden stairs that led to Iris's house above the salon. I knocked twice on the weather-beaten aluminum door.

86

Nothing.

"Try again," Aunt Shirley persisted.

I knocked again and waited a few seconds. Maybe we were too early and she wasn't home yet from running her errands. Peering inside the tiny-portioned glass in the door, I tried to see if I could glimpse any movement.

The kitchen was directly in front of me. All I could make out was the layout of the kitchen and doorway leading into what I guessed was the living room.

"Try the doorknob," Aunt Shirley said.

"Don't you dare!" Paige exclaimed. "That's illegal!"

I silently debated what I should do. Do I just leave without answers, or do I turn the knob and see what happens?

Ignoring Paige's gasp, I grasped the knob and turned. To my surprise the door opened. "Iris," I called out as we piled into her kitchen.

Nothing.

We were all three jammed into Iris's tiny sunshine yellow kitchen, trying to peer through the open doorway that led into her living room. There were no lights on, but I swore I caught the faint glow of the TV from her living room.

"I don't think we should be in here," Paige whispered. "Let's just go and come back later."

"No way," Aunt Shirley said as she pushed me out of her way and began walking through the doorway and into Iris's living room.

Praying Iris wouldn't be peeved that we'd just barged in, I hurried after Aunt Shirley. I could hear Paige trailing behind me and muttering under her breath.

Two steps into the living room I hit the back of Aunt Shirley. "Why'd you stop?" I asked.

"Look," Aunt Shirley said as she pointed to the floor.

Looking over her shoulder I let out a high-pitched girlie scream. I couldn't help it. I wasn't expecting to see Iris's body sprawled out on the carpet, her face covered in blood. Behind me I could hear Paige chanting, "Oh, my gosh! Oh, my gosh!"

Aunt Shirley knelt down and tried to find a pulse. Why I don't know. It was obvious Iris was dead.

Aunt Shirley stared into Iris's bloody mouth. "Looks like her tongue's been cut out. I'd say the killer put her on her back like this so she'd be sure to choke on her own blood. Panic her as she was dying."

"You think she was still alive when her tongue was cut out?" I asked, shocked at the thought of something so brutal.

"Yep. With all this blood, I'd say it was done while she was still alive. If it was done after she was dead, there wouldn't be as much blood."

"I think I'm going to go wait outside," Paige whispered.

"Don't touch anything!" Aunt Shirley shouted as Paige staggered her way through the kitchen and onto the deck.

"You know I'm gonna have to call Garrett and tell him what we found. He's going to flip when he finds out we went behind his back and came here."

Aunt Shirley snorted. "Suck it up, Buttercup."

I took out my cell phone and pulled up Garrett's number. Unfortunately for me, he actually answered. "Hey, Sin, kinda busy. What's up?"

I didn't know what to say, so I said nothing.

I could hear cursing on the other end. "First off, are you okay?"

"Yes."

"How bad is it?"

"You mean on a scale of one to dead body bad?" I don't know why I made it sound like a question.

More cursing. "Didn't I tell you to lay low today? What is it with you and attracting trouble?"

I couldn't help it...I started to cry.

"Don't cry, Sin," I heard Garrett sigh. "I'm sorry. Where are you? I'm coming now."

Between my ragged breath, hiccupping, and soft sobs, I told Garrett where I was. Hanging up the phone, I looked over at Aunt Shirley and Iris's dead body.

"That's what you went with?" Aunt Shirley scoffed. "Crying?"

"Shut up, Aunt Shirley," I said, trying to calm my nerves. I could hear the wailing of sirens in the background.

A few minutes later, Garrett came barging into the living room with Officer Chunsey and Officer Mike Ryan. Officer Ryan had recently left the Army and had only been with the Granville Police Department six months. He was a little over six feet tall, bald, and had muscles bulging everywhere. With his dark complexion and massive muscles, he always reminded me of Dwayne Johnson. The very intimidating Dwayne Johnson, not the laid-back-wide-grin Dwayne Johnson.

"Melvin should be here shortly to make the call," Officer Ryan informed us as he stared down at Iris. "So we have Garver's heart cut out, and now we have Iris's tongue cut out. That's quite a specific pattern."

"It is?" I asked.

"Agreed," Garrett said, ignoring my question.

"I'll start snapping pictures," Officer Ryan said.

It was obvious I wasn't going to get anywhere with the men. I turned and ambled down the narrow hallway toward the bedroom and bathroom area.

I had almost reached the bathroom when I heard Garrett yell out. "Where are you going? Don't touch anything!"

Without turning around I rolled my eyes. "I'm going to the bathroom." What he didn't know was that I was going to the bathroom to snoop around, not to actually use it.

It just so happened the first door I opened on the left side of the hallway was Iris's bedroom. Closing the door behind me I looked around, hoping to find some sort of clue. Her bed was centered against the wall closest to me, with a wooden headboard attached. On the far wall stood a tall oak dresser with four drawers, and next to her bed was a single oak nightstand.

I spotted a large notebook on the bed, and using the bottom of my shirt, I flipped it open. Bingo! It was her appointment book for the salon. Leafing through to October, I reached into my jeans and took out my cell phone. I quickly snapped a couple photos for the calendar month of October then shut the book, leaving it exactly where it was.

Deciding I had spent enough time snooping, and knowing Garrett would probably start looking for me, I opened the door and stepped into the hallway. Or more like stepped into Garrett. He was standing in the middle of the hall, arms crossed over his chest.

"I had better not find your fingerprints all over her bedroom."

"You won't."

"Find anything useful?" He was trying to sound stern, but I could see his lips twitching, trying not to smile.

I didn't say anything, just shook my head.

Dropping his arms to his side, Garrett stepped closer to me. "I'm sorry I yelled at you. It's been a while since I felt that scared. Hearing you cry, mentioning a dead body…it really got to me."

He leaned down and gave me a light kiss. Just a quick brush of his lips across mine, but the effect was like being squeezed to death by a boa constrictor.

But in a good way.

"I have to finish up here. I want to talk to the toxicology lab, have them check for something specific, then—"

"What specifically?" I couldn't help it. I had to know.

"Then," he continued, "I'll wrap it up as quick as I can and drop by your place tonight."

"You will?"

"Yes, Ryli, I will. I don't want you alone tonight."

Not only had he used my given name, but he invited himself over to my house tonight. I went into panic mode. What does my house look like? Had I picked up my underwear off the floor?

"How about you two quit making out in the hall and get over here and wrap up this dead body thing." God bless Aunt Shirley's big mouth.

Garrett turned and sauntered back down the hall and into the living room. I rushed down the hall after him, suddenly eager to print out the picture of the calendar on my phone before Garrett came over.

On an impulse, I decided to look in the sink. There were a number of dirty dishes with dried food caked on plastic plates, a pot that looked to have the remnants of macaroni and cheese stuck to the side, and lots of cups and silverware. Evidently keeping a clean kitchen wasn't high on Iris's list.

What did strike me as odd was the fact that sitting next to the sink were two clean mugs—like they had recently been washed and set there to dry. Just like at Dr. Garver's house.

Hopping into the Falcon, Aunt Shirley, Paige, and I drove to the newspaper to print out my picture. I had just unlocked the front door when Hank's truck came screeching to a halt in the tiny parking lot, gravel flying. Groaning, I knew what was coming next.

"I hear about a dead body discovered over the police scanner. Then minutes later I get a call from someone that it was *you* who discovered the body of the town's biggest gossip, and you don't call me to tell me?" Hank barked as he slammed the truck door shut.

"I'm sorry," I said sarcastically. "How stupid of me not to think to call you during my breakdown."

"How bad was it?"

"It was really bad," Paige whispered.

"Looks like someone cut out her tongue while she was still alive and waited for her to die," Aunt Shirley said. Leave it to Aunt Shirley to provide the truth.

Hank crossed his arm and glared at me. "What you seem to be forgetting lately is that it's your job to report on these matters, and you're lucky enough to be in the thick of it."

"Lucky enough?" I practically screamed. "Are you crazy? This has been the worst week of my life!"

Once again I felt the water works starting. What's wrong with me? Usually I thought of myself a little bit more put together than this. A couple dead bodies and suddenly I'm Simpering Sally.

"Leave her be you old coot," Aunt Shirley said. "Can't you see she's shaken up?"

Glaring at my aunt, Hank pushed us all through the glass double doors before locking the deadbolt behind him. That simple act had me even more upset. If Hank was taking safety precautions, I truly did have a lot to worry about.

"What'd you get?" Hank said as he held out his hand. "I figure you coming back here means you found something."

I debated on whether or not I should tell him, but then I figured maybe his seasoned eyes could help. Pulling the phone out of my pocket, I pulled up the gallery app and clicked on the photo. "I need to print this out. I found Iris' salon schedule on her bed and was able to snap pictures real quick before Garrett found me. I thought maybe Iris wrote down a name if she was expecting a visitor Sunday night or if someone was blackmailing her or something like that."

Hank took the phone and plugged it into the cord attached to the computer. "I knew you'd get something. Good work."

Paige leaned over and patted me on my shoulder. "See, you did good."

Hank's fingers flew over the keyboard. "I figure we help solve this murder alongside the police, papers will fly off the shelves."

A few seconds later and Hank had successfully blown up the October schedule to where we could all see it.

Bang! Bang!

I looked over and saw Mindy hopping up and down on her four-inch spiked stiletto heels banging on the glass doors. Her tiny body shivering in the cool night air.

Hank ran over to release the deadbolt in the center of the doors, flung them open, yanked her inside, and then rebolted the doors. "What're you doing out here? I told you to stay home."

"You're outta your mind, Hank Perkins, if you think I'm just gonna sit home twiddling my thumbs while you're solving a murder," Mindy said.

"Let's see what we got here," Aunt Shirley said.

It was basically a huge calendar with initials and abbreviations all over the place. No names were written out, but thinking back to who was in the salon that Friday morning after Dr. Garver's murder, I realized CH @ 8:30/t&s probably stood for Claire Hickman. I wasn't exactly sure what the 't&s' stood for.

"I think this here," I said pointing to Claire's name, "stands for Claire Hickman at eight-thirty. But I don't know what this 't&s' stands for."

"That probably stands for tease and style," Mindy said, patting her own poofy hair.

"It looks like that morning a lot of them were quickly penciled in," I said. "Notice how some are scribbled in with a pencil."

"I don't see an appointment for Sunday night," Hank grumbled.

"But there's a lot of scribble in the margins," Paige said. "Trying to figure this out could take a while."

"Mindy, since you seem to know this stuff, would you like to take it and decode it?" I asked.

"Yes!" Mindy grabbed the page up and did a victory dance.

Hank laughed and took her by the arm and guided her toward the front glass doors. "We're out," he said. "If you want a paycheck this week, get me something I can put in the paper." With that he slammed out of the office.

"Such a charmer," I muttered.

"Now that Mindy is on deciphering, what do we do next?" Paige asked.

"I think we should research paralytic drugs," I said.

"You think that's how the killer is doing it?" Aunt Shirley asked.

I nodded. "I really do. This is the second time Garrett has mentioned a toxicology report, and I keep seeing washed dishes at the crime scenes. When you take that into consideration with the fact that someone is overpowering these women without too much of a struggle, I think we should look into what drugs will specifically do that."

"I can help you do that," Paige said.

"Great idea," Aunt Shirley said. "Leaves me to just go home and go to bed."

I drove the girls back to their houses with the promise that we'd get together tomorrow afternoon to see what Paige was able to find out. I glanced at my watch and figured I still had an hour or so before Garrett would be at my place. I wrestled with what to change into the rest of the way home. I decided something sexy yet smart was needed.

Pulling into my drive, I cursed when the automatic porch light didn't go on. I'm not exactly sure when I noticed the pumpkin sitting on my steps leading into the house, mainly because I was too busy thinking about what I was going to have to clean before Garrett came by. It was one of those tall, thin pumpkins. Not even really my style. I liked my pumpkins small and round.

My first thought was Matt had finally gotten tired of me saying I would decorate for Halloween and just decided to do it himself. It had typical triangle eyes, but the mouth was hugely exaggerated and wide open. In fact, I could probably stick my hand inside the mouth to set the candle if I wanted.

I probably would have just walked right on by if I hadn't noticed the putrid smell. Had the pumpkin rotted already? Peering down, I noticed something hanging out of the pumpkin's mouth, resting on the jagged teeth. I reached out to touch it. The spongy rough texture took my breath away.

Realizing what I was touching, I jerked up and started screaming. Really I was just making soft whimpering sounds, but in my mind it was blood-curdling screams. I brought my hand up to cover my mouth.

Big mistake! That was the hand that just touched the tongue. I started to gag. Bending at the knees, as though that would help somehow, I tried sucking in air. Unfortunately that just put me closer to the nasty tongue.

Closing my eyes, I gave myself over to the inevitable. Standing up and running to the edge of the grass, I puked up what was left of the turkey sandwich I'd eaten for dinner. Not one to make the same mistake twice, I wiped my mouth with my shirt instead of my hand.

The soft scraping on my door made me look up. I could hear the distressful meowing of Miss Molly, followed by the scraping of her paws on the front door. She must have sensed my agony. I carefully walked up the three steps and reached for my keys when I saw the note stuck to the door with masking tape.

Not even caring that I was contaminating the scene, first with my vomit, and now by pulling the note off the door, I reached up and yanked the note down.

"The Bible says to watch your tongue and keep your mouth shut, and you will stay out of trouble. I guess Iris forgot that little bit of wisdom. Will you?"

Someone just declared war on me. Looking up from the note, I took in my surroundings.

My road doesn't get much traffic. It's a dead-end street off the beaten path of the main drag downtown. It's also partially secluded by two large oak trees in the front yard, with medium-sized shrubs lining the walkway into the house. I'd always felt safe here in my quaint cottage, but now I'd become an easy target for a crazy murderer.

Reaching into my pocket, I took out my phone and pulled up Garrett's number. I debated for a moment whether or not to call him and let him know what happened, or just tell him what he arrived. Knowing I'd never hear the end of it if I didn't tell him now, I pushed the send button and waited.

"Almost done here. What's up?"

I knew nothing I said was going to sound good to him. "Here's the thing. I was coming home from dropping off the girls, and I pulled into the driveway and saw a pumpkin. I thought maybe Matt had stopped by and decorated, so I didn't pay much attention." I hesitated a moment, choosing my words carefully.

"Go on." I heard the resignation in his voice, as though he already knew it wasn't going to be good.

"Well, I saw something sticking out of the pumpkin, so I reached down and touched it. It's a tongue. I'm assuming a human tongue. Maybe Iris's tongue."

"Son of a —" I pulled the phone away as Garrett continued his swearing. He ranted a minute before he finally calmed down. "Anything else besides the tongue?"

"Well," I said slowly, "there was a note taped to my front door basically saying it was Iris's tongue and that I better be careful or I'd end up the same way."

More swearing. I sat down on the front step, as far away from the pumpkin as I could get, and just waited for the storm to end. It didn't take long. "So, are you okay?"

I put the phone back to my ear. "I'm fine. Just sitting here on the front porch steps talking to you."

"You sound like you're in shock," Garrett said softly. "Sit tight. Don't go in the house until I get there. I'll be there in five. Think you'll be okay?"

I assured him I would be fine and hung up. I could still hear Miss Molly scraping and meowing. I felt guilty about not going in the house to comfort her, so I passed the time by talking to her through the door. I had just checked my phone to see what time it was when Garrett pulled into the driveway. Followed immediately by Officer Ryan.

I stood up and brushed off my jeans. Officer Ryan gave me a tight smile as he strode up the walkway carrying a small box. Smiling back I looked over at Garrett. He was not smiling. He looked angry and tired.

"It's in the pumpkin?" Officer Ryan asked.

"Yes. I didn't touch it again after the first time."

Bending down, Officer Ryan turned on his flashlight and inspected the tongue in the pumpkin. "Lots of blood on the back half here, which makes sense considering we believe Iris's tongue was cut out when she was still alive." He opened the box and took out gloves and a baggie.

Garrett flashed his beam of light onto the house. "I see they busted out your light. Would you mind if we opened the front door and turned on your light inside?" Garrett asked as he put on a set of gloves. "I want to fingerprint and finish processing the area."

"Of course. Let me just go put Miss Molly in my room so she doesn't escape."

I fished around in my jeans for my keys. When I pulled them out, Garrett took them from me and opened the door. Using his flashlight, he did a quick surveillance of my living room and the rest of the house, then motioned me inside. I bent down to scoop up the howling Miss Molly.

Garrett reached out and gave Molls a scratch behind her ear. The little minx started purring.

"I puked by the edge of the grass," I whispered in Miss Molly's fur.

Garrett leaned over and kissed my head. "I'll take care of it."

After dumping Molls on my bed, I began shoving dirty clothes in my hamper. Once that was done I sat down on the bed and unzipped my boots. My feet were beginning to hurt. I changed into flannel bottoms, a t-shirt, and warm fuzzy socks. I then went into the kitchen to brew some lavender tea. I also added a shot of whiskey to the mug.

Since my front door was open, I could hear bits and pieces of Garrett and Officer Ryan talking. Wrapping my hands around the warm lavender tea, I sank down into my couch to eavesdrop. Unfortunately, most of what they were saying was about lab and processing, not anything too useful. I set the mug down on the end table and closed my eyes.

"Ryli, wake up."

I felt Garrett rocking me awake. I opened my eyes and stared at him. He looked exhausted. His eyes were bloodshot and his face was lined. But even after being on the job for over ten hours, dealing with a dead body and dead body parts, he still looked good enough to kiss.

"We're finished, and I'm beat. I need to rest a bit. Go on back to your room, and I'll stay here on the couch. I don't want you alone tonight."

"I can't have you sleeping on the couch," I said. "It's not that comfortable."

Garrett smiled. "Ryli, I spent years in the military. Did a couple tours in Afghanistan. We didn't always have beds. Believe me, the couch will be fine."

I still felt guilty leaving him to sleep on the couch while I got the bed. But I also knew better than to argue.

CHAPTER 10

I woke early and made my way to the living room. It was empty. I should have known Garrett would be out the door before I even stirred from bed. I found a note on the counter.

"Unfortunately I can't keep you locked up in your house. Please be careful today. Hopefully last night's stunt will help narrow my suspects, and this will be over soon. I'll call you later."

He was narrowing suspects down? I needed to get a move on if I was going to solve this case. It was after nine o'clock, and I still hadn't even gotten out of bed. I couldn't believe how long I had slept. Or better yet, how well I had slept.

I scurried over to my closet and yanked on a pair of jeans and a sweatshirt. In less than fifteen minutes I had completed my morning ritual of bathroom break, teeth brushed, hair pulled into a ponytail, and Miss Molly fed.

I called Paige and told her to be ready. I was coming over and had major news to tell her. I also asked her to call Aunt Shirley and tell her we'd be there shortly, I had a lead. I didn't wait for her reply.

A few minutes later I walked into Paige's house. I never knock. Best friends don't have to. Unfortunately, when you don't knock you have to be prepared for anything. Today it was Matt standing in Paige's kitchen cooking breakfast.

"Wow. I don't even know what to say," I said.

Matt smiled and started putting food on plates. Never one to pass up food, I grabbed one of the plates and started shoving food in my mouth. I realized I was starving after having lost everything in my stomach the night before.

"Paige, let's go," I yelled out. "I have news."

"You aren't the only one," Matt said as he finished putting the breakfast on the plates.

I was going to ask him what he meant when Paige walked into the kitchen. She looked like her normal million-dollar self, but I could sense something was different. She smiled at me and kissed me on the cheek.

Whoa…okay. Something was really up.

"You know, it's rude to call someone without saying hello or goodbye, just barking orders and hanging up," Paige said as she picked up the plate of food and began eating.

I was going to tell her to get over herself when I saw it. I mean, how could I not? It practically blinded me! A whopping two-and-a-half carat, white gold, princess-cut diamond engagement ring. At least that's what it looked like at a quick glance.

I screamed, threw the plate of food down on the counter, and sprinted over to where she was casually standing. I yanked the food out of her hands and shoved it at Matt. "When did this happen?"

"Last night, after you dropped me off from Iris's house. Matt came by after he heard what happened."

Had that only been last night? So much had transpired in between Iris's house and right now. Namely, I'd had a human tongue put in my Halloween pumpkin and Garrett had spent the night.

"The minute I heard about what happened at Iris's place," Matt said, "I realized I was being stupid carrying around this ring, waiting for what I thought needed to be the right time. This was the right time. I don't know how I'd live if something happened to Paige before I had a chance to tell her how I felt. How I've felt for a long time now."

Paige and I erupted into shouts and screams. This is exactly what we'd always planned when we were younger...becoming sisters. "How did Mom take it?"

"We went over early this morning to tell her," Matt said.

"She was so excited! She even cried a little when I showed her the ring," Paige gushed.

"Did you still want to go with me today?" I asked. "Or did you have to go see your parents to tell them the news?"

"Oh, no. We already told them this morning, too," Paige assured me.

Had they been up since before dawn?

"Did you call Aunt Shirley and tell her we were on our way?" I asked.

"I'd really like it if you didn't get my future bride killed today," Matt said with a pointed look at me.

"Geez, what is it with everyone thinking I'm going to get them or me killed today?" I asked.

Paige laughed at my question. "Did you already get a lecture from Garrett about being on your best behavior today?"

"Yes," I pouted. "Look, I'm not going to do anything to jeopardize your future wife, who also happens to be my best friend, and hopefully the mother of my nieces and nephews someday. So give it a rest." I could see the last part had Matt fretting.

So I'd hit a nerve with the baby remark. Good, let him stew a while thinking about screaming babies and dirty diapers and sleepless nights. Wasn't anything he didn't deserve for leaving me out of his wedding plans.

Paige swatted Matt on the arm as she gathered up her things. "Stop nagging your sister. We'll be careful." She leaned in and kissed his cheek. "I'll be home in time for dinner. How about we celebrate with some steaks tonight?"

That perked Matt right up. "Sounds good, babe. I don't get off until around eight o'clock, but I'm all for a late dinner."

"I may even whip up a chocolate surprise for dessert."

That really perked Matt up.

"And maybe some champagne to celebrate," I said. "Might as well get that in now, because once she's knocked up, no more boozy celebrations."

Matt scowled at me as I laughed. Oh, this was going to be so much fun...endless hours of torture.

"How about I get married before you get me knocked up?" Paige reprimanded.

A few minutes later, Paige and I jumped in the Falcon and headed out to Oak Grove Manor to get Aunt Shirley. We called to let her know we were on our way so she'd be waiting for us outside. I figured I'd just let them both know at the same time what had happened last night, since Paige's announcement was more important. And I will admit I was afraid Matt might flip his lid if he knew about the tongue, especially since I was taking Paige with me to investigate.

Once Aunt Shirley was in the Falcon, I headed for Burger Barn. The place was only slightly busy, so we were able to find a parking spot close to the front door.

"Go grab us a booth and I'll get drinks," I told Aunt Shirley and Paige. I placed the order, got the empty cups, then started filling them one at a time. Burger Barn has one of those "squirt" machines where you can make any kind of soda drink you want, which is totally cool. I put a couple squirts of cherry and vanilla in all of them, and then carefully carried the drinks to the booth.

As Paige started taking a drink, Aunt Shirley reached out and grabbed her hand. "What's this? The boy finally decided to buy the cow?" She cackled at her own crass joke.

I bristled, but Paige nodded. "Yep. Said after what happened to me yesterday at Iris's house, he couldn't imagine living without me."

"Well, good for him for finally coming around," Aunt Shirley said.

Aunt Shirley was happy with this? I always figured for some reason she didn't like Paige and that's why she gave her such a hard time about "giving it away" to my brother. Who knew she was more upset over Matt's actions than Paige's.

"Speaking of what happened yesterday," I said. "The reason I called us together today was because I have to tell you what happened after I got home last night from dropping you all off."

"You and Barney Fife finally hook up?" Aunt Shirley said.

I looked around in a panic hoping no one had heard. "Don't be silly! I mean, yes, he did come over—"

"I knew it!" Paige cried, practically jumping up and down in the vinyl seat.

"Does this mean I'm the only woman at this table not getting any?" Aunt Shirley asked.

Perish the thought!

I help up my hand. "Just listen. When I pulled up in the drive last night, I noticed a pumpkin on my front porch stairs. I thought Matt had come over to decorate, since I obviously haven't gotten around to it yet. When I got closer, I could tell something wasn't right. It had one of those extra-wide carved mouths with sharp teeth, and something was sticking out of it."

Aunt Shirley sucked in her breath. "Tell me it wasn't…"

"Wait, what?" Paige said, looking back and forth between the two of us. "What did I miss?"

"Yep. It was Iris's tongue," I said.

"What?" Paige cried, choking a little on her cherry vanilla cola. "Are you serious? Why on Earth didn't you mention this to Matt this morning?"

I debated on what to say. This was the first time it actually hit me that my best friend was now marrying my brother, so I wasn't exactly sure where her allegiance would lie. Would it make a difference on what Matt said whether or not she helped me out from now on? Not that I planned on finding more dead bodies, but one never knows.

"Oh, pooh," Aunt Shirley said, giving me a knowing look. "I'm sure Ryli didn't want to ruin your big moment."

I mouthed a silent thank you to Aunt Shirley as Paige stared lovingly at her ring. I had to give it to Aunt Shirley, she was amazingly astute on reading people. She probably was an awesome private investigator back in her day. I admit I sometimes just thought she was making herself out to be something bigger than she really was, but now I'm beginning to think I was totally selling her short.

"So, what happened after you found the tongue?" Aunt Shirley asked.

"Yes, what happened?" echoed Paige.

I filled them in on finding the Bible verse, calling Garrett, he and Officer Ryan coming out and processing the scene.

"So I'm thinking our next lead is with the note. It had a Bible verse on it. I mean, I don't know who the killer is, but I know someone we can ask about the quote. I was thinking we should go see Pastor Williams today. Maybe he can shed some light on this."

"Sounds good to me," Aunt Shirley said as she slid out of the booth.

I phoned Pastor Williams and asked him if we could stop by real quick. I told him I had some Bible questions I was hoping he could answer. Pastor Williams assured me we would be more than welcomed, and to come by the parsonage at our convenience.

Our church bought the current parsonage about five years ago. The old parsonage used to be right next to the church, but recent trends have encouraged churches to buy away from the church, giving the pastor and family a little more privacy. So our church raised money and bought a three-bedroom, ranch-style brick house over on Locust Drive. I'd only been in the parsonage one other time in all these years.

I rang the doorbell and waited for the door to be opened. To say I was nervous would be an understatement. It felt like I was waiting to see the principal.

"I hope this goes fast," Aunt Shirley said. "These places always give me the willies."

I was about to ask her why they give her the willies when the door opened. Instead of Pastor Williams, it was Sister Williams that answered the door. She looked like she was in mourning in her black wool skirt and black oversized sweater. Her brown wavy hair was pulled back in a bun so tight that it distorted her features slightly. She looked older than her fifty plus years.

"Ladies, please come in. Pastor Williams is expecting you." Was I the only one that thought it weird she referred to her husband as Pastor Williams?

She led us through the sparse living room and into Pastor Williams' study. Compared to the drab living room, this room was actually quite lovely. It had boxed, wooden paneling on all four walls, and three built-in bookshelves located around the room. There was a large, oak desk along one wall, with two beige wingback chairs in front of the desk. Along another wall sat a beige two-person loveseat with two white pillows placed on either end of the loveseat. Pastor Williams sat behind the desk in a large, throne-like leather chair.

"Ladies, welcome," Pastor Williams said as he gestured around the room. "Please sit wherever you like." He continued sitting while we volleyed for places to sit. Aunt Shirley and I sat in the chairs in front of his desk, while Paige elected to sit on the loveseat to my right.

Pastor Williams was a large man. He stood over six feet tall and probably weighed over two hundred and fifty pounds. I'd also guess he played football at some point in his life. But now in his fifties, you could see the lines in his face, the gray scattered throughout his hair.

Sister Williams waited until we were seated before asking if we'd like something to drink. Since we'd just come from Burger Barn, we all said no.

"Do you mind if I sit in, or is this private?" Sister Williams asked.

I didn't see the big deal in having her sit in. "Of course. We really just had some questions about the Bible."

"Well, that's what I'm here for," Pastor Williams said. "Ask away."

I looked over at Aunt Shirley. I wasn't sure if she wanted me to start or if she wanted to start, seeing as how she had years of P.I. training. She nodded for me to go ahead and take the lead.

"I'm not sure how much you know about what's been going on with the murders, but—"

"Oh, such a tragic thing," Pastor Williams said. "We've been beside ourselves here." He looked over to where Sister Williams sat demurely on the couch next to Paige. "You know Dr. Garver was not only a personal friend, but also on our church board. We were devastated when we heard the news. As you know, we are holding Dr. Garver's memorial service on Thursday." He sounded as though hosting her memorial service was some kind of great honor.

"What about Iris's death?" I asked. "What do you know about it?"

I saw his quick frown when I mentioned Iris's name.

"I'm afraid I don't know anything relevant as far as *that woman* is concerned," Pastor Williams said. I could hear the condemnation in his voice as clear as a bell. I surreptitiously glanced at Aunt Shirley to see if she caught it. I could tell by her one raised eyebrow she had.

"Do you know how she was murdered?" I asked.

"No. And I'm not sure how her murder would have anything to do with Dr. Garver's murder. I mean those women couldn't be more different. One was an educated, pillar of the community and her church...the other a gossiping whoremonger."

My mouth dropped. I knew the word whoremonger was in the Bible, I'd just never heard anyone use it before. "Well, I'm assuming since Dr. Garver's murder was the first murder we've had in this town in I don't know how many years, then immediately afterward we have Iris's murder, they must be related somehow, don't you think?"

"What does all this have to do with the Bible reference you needed?" Pastor Williams asked, as though he was tiring of our presence.

I narrowed my eyes at him. "I'm not sure if you know this, but we are the ones that found Iris's body."

"Oh, you poor girls!" Sister Williams moaned from the loveseat.

Pastor Williams looked shaken. "No, I wasn't aware."

"Do you know how Iris died?" I asked.

"No," Pastor Williams said. "No one has said anything to me. She wasn't a church goer, so the other preachers in town haven't said anything to me about what they know."

Well now, that's interesting.

"Her tongue was cut out," I said.

I heard Sister Williams gasp. I turned my head and saw her wringing her hands together in distress. "After this is all over, please come and talk with us about this," Sister Williams said. "We can help you."

Help me with what exactly?

Pastor Williams nodded. "Yes. Any time you want to talk, I'm here for you."

Okay. This awkward fest needed to end soon or I was going to start screaming. Time to get this over with.

"When I got home last night, someone had planted Iris's tongue on my front porch along with a note."

I saw Sister Williams get up from the loveseat and start pacing back and forth. She was chewing on her lower lip, and I couldn't be sure, but I think she was praying.

Pastor Williams cleared his throat. "What did the note say?"

I wasn't sure how much I should tell him. I mean, I'm pretty sure Garrett would be mad if I blabbed all over town there was a note, but I thought maybe I could cover it up with the fact Pastor Williams *was* my preacher, so he probably couldn't talk about it.

Who was I kidding? He just acknowledged a while ago he talked with other preachers about people. I looked over at Aunt Shirley to see what she thought. She gave me a slight nod, so I continued. "The note told me the Bible says to watch your tongue and keep your mouth shut and you'll stay out of trouble. Then it went on to say that Iris had forgotten that admonition and that I had better watch my step or else the same thing would happen to me."

Pastor Williams's face went pale. "I'm not sure what I should be saying here. I mean, it's bad enough Dr. Garver was murdered, but this is incomprehensible. Does Chief Kimble know of this?"

"Of course. I called him the minute I found the tongue and he came over to gather clues."

"Sister Williams, are you okay?" Paige asked.

I looked over at Sister Williams. She was bent over at the waist, taking deep breaths. I know she's perceived as being a gentle soul and all that, but I really wasn't prepared for her to actually start hyperventilating on me. Time to wrap this gabfest up.

Ignoring Sister Williams I pressed on. "So what do you think? This is from the Bible, right?"

"Yes," Pastor Williams said, his skin still pale. "I don't know for sure, but I'd say you can eliminate your 'King James only' people as the killer, since it's not a King James translation. Maybe I should let Chief Kimble know about that when I see him today."

"You're meeting with him?" I asked.

"Well, he's meeting with the whole Ministerial Alliance committee. I guess he wants our help in the investigation."

Or he's secretly getting your alibis.

Pastor Williams frowned at me. "With everything I've seen and heard the last few days, I'd definitely watch my step if I were you. It sounds as if you're too close for your own good."

"Ha!" Aunt Shirley barked. "Never you mind about Ryli's safety. We got her back."

Pastor Williams cleared his throat and shifted in his chair. "Well, then I guess all I can tell you is it sounds like a New Living Translation. As far as what it means, I think it's self-explanatory. Especially when you take into consideration the fact it was written

112

about Iris. I mean, was there really a bigger gossiper than her? I'll admit I hated the fact my wife went to her to get her hair done." He turned to glower at his wife. "It's always bothered me my wife gave that woman a dime of our money."

While I'd never considered myself a friend of Iris's, I sure wasn't going to sit here and listen to this hatred much longer. The judgment coming from my preacher's mouth was appalling. Talk about seeing someone in a new light.

"It wasn't all that bad," Sister Williams said as she sat back down on the couch next to Paige. "Iris did have some good qualities."

"Whatever you say," Pastor Williams grumbled. "You knew her better than I did."

"Thank you for your time." Aunt Shirley stood up. "You've been a great help to us today."

Paige, Aunt Shirley, and I walked out with Sister Williams. "Ladies, please understand my husband is under a lot of stress. With Dr. Garver's passing, it means we have to fill another place on the board. Plus the fact we are doing the memorial service and the hours of prep work that entails, and he still needs to get ready for Thursday's memorial service, the Fall Festival, and Sunday's church service. Well, he's very stressed."

Stressed? It was all I could do not to laugh out loud. Is that what they're calling narrow-mindedness these days? Because it sure sounded to me like he was judging Iris big time.

As I followed Aunt Shirley and Paige out the front door, Sister Williams touched my arm. "Ryli, please don't forget you signed up to help get the games and booths around on Friday."

I groaned inwardly. I'd forgotten all about it.

I looked into the heartfelt, pleading eyes of my pastor's wife, then down to the hand that clung to me like a life support.

"Of course I remember," I said, the lie rolling off my tongue.

"How about three o'clock at the church? Just knowing you and the other ladies will be there to help is such a relief."

I gave her a weak smile and told her I was looking forward to it. I'm sure she saw right through me, but being the bigger person she elected not to say anything. Instead Sister Williams patted my arm and smiled.

CHAPTER 11

"What did she want?" Aunt Shirley demanded as I got into the Falcon and pulled out of the driveway.

"To remind me I signed up this Friday to set up booths for the festival," I said, hating the whine I heard in my voice.

I looked in the rear-view mirror and saw Paige gazing wistfully at her engagement ring. "Thinking about the wedding?"

Paige sighed. "I was thinking I've always known Pastor Williams was an arrogant SOB, but today he *really* sounded like a jerk."

Aunt Shirley laughed. "Well, you gotta remember he's just a man. He puts his pants on one leg at a time just like other men do."

"I guess," Paige mumbled. "Doesn't make it any easier, though. Just think, he's the one we're going to have to go to for marriage counseling and all that."

"Well, the wife totally gives me the willies with all that whimpering and wringing of her hands," Aunt Shirley said.

I looked over at Aunt Shirley to see if she was serious. "She's been like that since I've known her. And I've practically known her my whole life."

"Still, I don't like it. She needs to be more..." Aunt Shirley trailed off.

"More like you?" I asked.

"Exactly!"

We decided to make a pit stop at the newspaper since I had to write up a piece in the paper about Iris's death. Obviously I was going to leave out the part about coming home to her tongue on my front porch stuck in a Halloween pumpkin.

The front door chimed as we walked into the main area of the building. Mindy was sitting behind her desk, lazily leafing through a gossip magazine. Today she had on hot pink Capri pants with an off-the-shoulder aqua cropped sweater, and neon-pink, patent leather pumps from Jimmy Choo. The four-inch heels were so teeny tiny they were like icepicks.

Sashaying effortlessly over to where we were, she gave me a small squeeze around my waist. "Hank had to run to Kansas City today, so it's just us girls. I've heard rumors about Iris's tongue missing, is it true?"

"Sort of," I said.

Mindy patted my hand. "Don't say another word. How about I make us some hot tea and we talk about it?"

"How about you bring out something stronger?" Aunt Shirley said.

Mindy laughed. "Go ahead and sit, the water is already hot. Just give me a second."

We watched her stroll over to the buffet and prepare the cups. I was about to stand up and go help when she turned around with two mugs looped in each hand…still walking on those icepicks. I figured she was fine without my help.

We each reached for a mug when Mindy started squealing. "You got engaged!" She set down her mug and lifted Paige's hand. "Oh, yes, Matt did good." She turned the ring side to side. I had a sudden vision of Mindy as Gollum whispering, "My precious."

116

Paige's eyes filled with tears. "Yes. Matt did good."

"So when's the big day?" Mindy demanded.

"We haven't set a date yet."

"Speaking of dates," Mindy said, "I've been decoding the ledger from the salon. I have a list of people at the salon the day after Dr. Garver died, and I've even compiled a list of people who were there for the whole month of October. I believe I have everyone accounted for and what they were doing at the salon. However, I'm just not sure if it helps any. The notes in the margin really didn't help me on who might be blackmailing or threatening Iris."

"That was fast," I said, impressed at what she'd been able to accomplish in so little time. "And don't worry, every little thing helps."

I spent the next hour writing up a piece for the paper about Iris's death. Then we sat around and theorized about who would have motive to kill two women who had virtually nothing in common. Pastor Williams was right. I didn't think these women hung out together. They didn't attend church together. Outside of probably shopping at the same grocery store here in town and Dr. Garver getting her hair done at Legends, they really had no cause to run into each other.

We ordered in sandwiches from a local café that delivers and talked about wedding plans. Mainly Mindy and Paige talked. Aunt Shirley and I just listened.

Or rather I half listened. I couldn't help but think about Garrett and what kind of information he was getting from the Ministerial Alliance. Was he seriously thinking that one of the preachers in town was the killer just because the threatening note left to me referenced the Bible?

* * *

I dropped Aunt Shirley off first then I drove Paige home. I was getting ready to pull out of her driveway when she tapped on my window. "Hey, why don't you and Garrett come over around eight-thirty for dessert and drinks?"

I must have looked confused because Paige laughed and said, "C'mon, this is the perfect opportunity to call him!"

"Don't you want to be alone with Matt tonight? I thought this was a celebration dinner?"

"We have the whole night to celebrate," Paige giggled. "I'm making my chocolate lava cake."

"Sold," I said.

My mom is a creature of habit, so I knew I'd find her in the library curled up on her chaise reading a mystery in front of her gas fireplace. As a little girl I loved sitting in this room with her. I'd be reading *The Baby-Sitters Club* while she'd read her mysteries. As I got older, I'd read what she was reading just to be closer to her.

Not wanting to startle her, I watched her silently from the doorframe. She looked peaceful, lounging in her pale pink maxi dress, her long blonde hair braided halfway down her back, and her bare feet tucked in next to her. She had a cup of hot tea on the round end table next to the chaise.

I knocked softly on the frame. "Hey, Mom."

My mom jerked her head up and narrowed her eyes at me. "About time you were getting here, young lady. I had to hear about it from Myrtle down at the grocery store that you found Iris's body!"

Ut oh!

"Sorry. It was really crazy after finding the body." I proceeded to tell her about the tongue and concluded with what happened this morning at the Williams' house. I conveniently left out the part about Garrett staying the night.

For the longest time Mom didn't say anything. Finally she stood up from her reclining position and opened her arms to me. I practically ran to her. No matter how old you get, there's nothing like the comfort of your mother's arms when you need them.

"I'm stuck. I was hoping you'd tell me a little about Dr. Garver and your thoughts on who might have killed her." I held my breath, hoping she wouldn't discourage me.

Mom sighed. "Let me guess, you're trying to solve this. I blame myself. After all, there's nothing I love more than a good murder mystery."

I gave her my sweetest smile and batted my eyes, making her laugh. "Let's hear what you have so far."

I spent the next fifteen minutes telling her everything I knew and could remember, including gossip and conversations with people around town. I told her Garrett had met with the Ministerial Alliance, and how I suspected it was to pick their brain and to see about alibies.

This took Mom by surprise. "He thinks it might be a preacher?"

"I don't know. I think he's not leaving anything to chance."

Mom was silent for a few minutes. "I guess in some ways that makes sense."

"I'm not sure how the killer is doing it. I think it might be a drug or something. I overheard Garrett mention getting toxicology reports from the lab. Maybe the killer is drugging the women and that's how he's overpowering them?"

"Could be," Mom mused.

Deciding to steer Mom away so she didn't get too upset over my involvement, I asked her about her duties for the memorial service and the church carnival.

"I have a dessert and side dish to make for the memorial service Thursday. Thankfully I got out of setting up on Friday. I just have to bring in decorated cupcakes Friday afternoon."

"I'm on the Friday afternoon game set up," I said.

Mom smiled. "It'll do you good. It's time for the younger generation to step up and help us old timers out."

I grunted. "I suppose."

"You haven't asked me about the surprise this morning."

"Geez! I'm a horrible sister and best friend. I keep forgetting!"

Mom laughed. "You just have a lot on your plate."

I stayed and chatted with Mom about the wedding for a little while longer, then decided it was time to bite the bullet and call Garrett.

CHAPTER 12

I hadn't spent any quality time with Miss Molly in forever, so I decided to go home. Pulling into the driveway, I couldn't help but feel apprehensive. After all, the last time I did this, I had a dead woman's tongue greet me at my front door.

Luckily for me, the only thing greeting me at the door this time was the mail and Miss Molly. She followed me into the kitchen and watched intently as I refilled her water bowl. As though somehow I might mess that task up.

I tried calling Garrett twice, and both times it went straight to voicemail. I was pretty sure he was avoiding my calls. I was just about to call again when my ringer went off.

Unfortunately, it wasn't Garrett but Aunt Shirley.

"What's up?" I asked.

Silence…then a subtle wheezing.

"Put that thing down and talk to me!" I yelled.

"Don't get your knickers in a wad," Aunt Shirley said. I heard a drawer shut. "So, I've been thinking. I think we should get hold of Janice and see what she knows about these murders. She was Iris's best friend. If anyone knows something, it'd be her."

I had to admit it was a pretty good idea.

"Do you think she'll talk with us?" I asked.

"I already called her. She said we can come by tonight around seven."

Shirley and I could question Janice, and I'd still have plenty of time to drive out to the farm for dessert. "I'll pick you up at six forty-five."

I decided a nap was in order. I had just started drifting when my cell phone rang. Groaning, I glanced over to see who was calling and quickly answered.

"I see you've been trying to call," Garrett said by way of greeting. "Everything okay?"

I tried to think of a way to ask what he learned at the Ministerial Alliance meeting without being obvious, but nothing came to mind. "Have you spoken with Matt today?" I asked.

"Nope. Been swamped here working on the murders."

I decided to rip off the Band-Aid. "Well, Matt asked Paige to marry him last night, and they want to know if we want to come over tonight for a celebratory dessert and drinks."

Silence.

I knew I was holding my breath but I couldn't help it. No matter how old you get, asking a guy out never gets easier.

"I have to say, I'm a little shocked," Garrett chuckled. "Of all the things I was expecting you to say, this wasn't one of them."

I hoped that was a good thing.

"What time?" he asked.

I couldn't stop the grin from spreading over my face. "About eight-thirty. Do you think you will be done by then?"

"I think I will be. I'm still checking alibis right now from my meeting today. Most of the information I'm waiting on won't come in for a few days, so I should be wrapped up by eight-thirty."

Don't ask! Don't ask!

"How about I pick you up around eight," Garrett said. "Maybe we can have a celebratory drink at your place before we head over."

I suddenly remembered my date with Aunt Shirley and Janice. I didn't want to risk Garrett showing up early at my place and me not being here. And I sure the heck didn't want to tell him what I was really doing.

"How about I pick *you* up at eight o'clock, and we have a drink at *your* house?" I asked.

"Why?" I could tell he was instantly suspicious.

"No reason. It's the twenty-first century for crying out loud." I hated how defensive I sounded. "A girl can pick up a guy at his house and have drinks."

"Uh huh," he said, not believing a word I said. "Okay, I'll let you play this out. I'll see you at my house at eight."

I hung up my cell phone and decided to forgo the nap. I figured if I was going to get Garrett's attention, it was time to step up my game. I went to my closet and looked through my clothes. It was time to pull out the big guns.

* * *

I twirled in front of the mirror, admiring the finished product. I have to say, I felt pretty darn good. I'd decided to go with my burgundy, long-sleeved sweater dress. It had a slim, silver chain belt that gave my waist definition. The dress stopped above my knees, so I opted for my knee-high brown suede boots with no heel. I put a few curls in my hair to give it some volume, and even took time for eye shadow and mascara.

By the time I finished getting ready, I was about five minutes late picking up Aunt Shirley. I could tell by the way she was tapping her foot outside the Manor that she wasn't happy.

"You're late!" she said as she folded herself into the front seat of the Falcon. She turned to look at me and whistled under her breath. "Why you lookin' so good? It's just Janice."

I smiled at her compliment. Glad to know someone else thought I was looking good. "I'm meeting up with Garrett after this to go out to Paige's."

Aunt Shirley looked me up and down again, and then buckled her seatbelt. "It'll do."

Janice lived on Tipton Street. It was located on the outskirts of town, going south, but still in city limits. It was one of the seedier parts to live in Granville. The dilapidated houses were spaced about fifty feet apart, with junk and broken toys littering the front yards. The majority of the houses were all leaning precariously, with large spots of randomly chipped off paint. There were a few that were even missing windows. This was not a street I went down unless I had to. And it's definitely not a street I went down at night.

"I hope she has something good to tell us," I said as we got out of the Falcon and headed toward the tiny, paint-chipped house. Aunt Shirley and I straddled car parts and beer cans near the carport. Guess her husband, Tom, couldn't be bothered to throw away the cans.

Classy.

I reached over to help Aunt Shirley up the ramshackled wooden steps, but she waved me off. Reaching the door first, I knocked on a door that looked like it couldn't keep the wind out, much less an intruder.

I could hear a TV blaring inside the house, so I knew someone was home. I waited a few more minutes then knocked again.

"Janice, answer the door!" a male voice shout.

A few seconds later Aunt Shirley and I were greeted with a bright light snapping on over our heads and the door swung open.

"Hi, guys. Come on in," Janice said leading us into the house.

The front door opened up into a time warp...also known as the living room. Tom was sitting on a sofa that was straight out of the 70s—dark wooden frame with huge orange and brown flowers. And if I wasn't mistaken, there was a cottage or something hidden sporadically in the pattern. A dark, heavy oak coffee table with two orange hinged doors sat flanked by two velvet chairs done in a burnt orange. I *barely* resisted running my hand over the velvet. I'd never seen anything so amazing, yet hideous. The burnt orange glass ceiling light fixture was the pièce de résistance.

"Hey Tom," I greeted.

Tom didn't look up from the television, but he did grunt as he lifted the beer to his lips.

"Let's just go in the kitchen," Janice said quickly.

We followed her through a doorway to our right that led into another time warp. I shook my head. Was this for real? Who doesn't update their house...ever.

The kitchen was extremely dark and dingy. It was done in the same burnt orange and brown colors, but with an addition of gold and avocado green. The cabinets were a dark wood with even darker handles. The linoleum flooring with the different sized rectangles of orange, gold, and cream just about gave me vertigo. The wallpaper was a mixture of huge burnt yellow and orange flowers with green leaves, and the dishwasher and other appliances sitting out were all avocado green.

Janice motioned for us to take a seat at the avocado green Formica table. Aunt Shirley and I pulled out the matching avocado green metal chairs and sat down. Janice walked over with a large ceramic cookie jar with a mushroom motif on the front. She plunked it down on the table and opened the lid.

I expected the cookies to be left over from 1970. She reached in and handed us each a chocolate chip cookie.

"Would you both like some lemonade?" Janice asked.

Lemonade and chocolate chip cookies? "No thanks."

"We were wondering if you could maybe shed some light on Iris's death for us," Aunt Shirley said.

Janice didn't say anything at first. She just sat chewing her cookie, her eyes filling with tears.

"I have no idea who would do this to Iris," Janice said when she finished her cookie. "I mean, yes, she liked to gossip and all, but she didn't deserve to die like she did just because of a little gossip. I mean, someone cut out her tongue!"

Janice started sobbing loudly, tears flowing down her cheeks. Aunt Shirley rummaged through her purse and handed Janice some tissue. Janice dabbed at her cheeks while she continued sobbing. While I felt sorry for her, I really didn't have time for theatrics. I needed answers, and then I needed to get back in time for my date with Garrett.

"Do you know what it was Iris had on Dr. Garver?" I asked, hoping to distract her so she'd stop crying.

Janice dabbed one more time at her cheeks before answering. "I don't know everything. Iris was real good about keeping the really juicy parts to herself—for leverage, ya know?"

I nodded my head. "Of course."

"Sometimes she'd give specifics. Like last week Patty Carter came in yelling about how she'd just heard Dr. Garver was cutting funding next year to the basketball teams to give more money to the football team so they could get new uniforms and equipment. Now, whether or not it's true, Patty Carter believed it. And according to Iris, she was steaming mad. Patty's nephew, Michael, is on the boys' basketball team, and she said it would be over her dead body before his sport was cut funding."

Patty Carter. Hadn't she been in Iris's salon the day after Dr. Garver's murder? But why kill Iris? Was she afraid Iris may tell people what she'd said? Obviously others knew, so killing her would be unnecessary. Still, it was something to go on.

"Then there was the time Dr. Garver refused to let the Booster Club do their annual fundraiser. Kim Baker was the president, and I actually witnessed that meltdown in the salon." Janice blew her nose on a wadded up tissue. "She was so mad, she was actually shaking." She laughed and hiccupped at the same time.

Maybe this wasn't going to be as easy as I thought. Something told me we could be here all night listening to the number of grievances Iris knew about when it came to Dr. Garver.

It was fifteen minutes to eight before we finally left Janice's house.

"What do you think?" I asked as I drove Aunt Shirley back to the Manor. "Should we question Patty and Kim?"

"I think we can find a ton of stories about people hating Dr. Garver. The best lead I think we got would be to question Patty. I'm not sure how she fits with killing Iris. Seems to me the killer should have just kept *their* mouth shut if the motive for killing Iris was to shut *Iris* up."

I nodded my head in agreement.

I pulled up under the awning to let Aunt Shirley out. "Make sure you put that dress to good use tonight. I don't want you moping about the next few days...not when we have a murder to solve."

I was glad the car was dark enough to hide my blush. Or I thought it was until Aunt Shirley started laughing. "Ain't no shame in a woman wanting to remember she's a woman."

As I peeled out of the circle drive I could still hear Aunt Shirley cackling.

CHAPTER 13

Garrett lives five miles from town out in the country. The house itself was a ranch-style home with a loft. He had seven acres, with a one-acre pond behind the house. The first thing Garrett did when he bought the house a year ago was build a two-car garage Morton building to the left side of his brick and vinyl house. The façade of the Morton building was made to match his house.

I grabbed my purse and got out of the Falcon. I made sure there were no wrinkles in my sweater dress, and carefully made my way to the large mahogany door with beveled glass and sidelights. I was about to knock on the door when Garrett beat me to the punch.

And a punch is exactly how to describe what I felt when he opened the imposing door. He had on dark, loose-fitting jeans with a black, long-sleeved fitted t-shirt. He stepped back to let me in then quietly closed the door behind me. I was suddenly very nervous.

He leaned over and kissed my cheek. "You look beautiful, Sin."

I was getting used to the nickname.

I followed Garrett through the extra-wide doorframe, and into the main living area of the house. The enormous living room had panoramic floor-to-ceiling windows built into the back and right side walls. You could see the beautiful view of the one-acre pond and woods behind the house. The wall to my left housed a stone fireplace with a large wood beam as the mantle. The exposed beam ceiling and curved wooden staircase almost directly behind me that led up to the loft and bathroom gave this part of the house a log-cabin feel.

The lighting in the room was soft and romantic. From one of the exposed beams in the center of the room Garrett had a suspended wagon wheel with six dimly lit mason jars hanging from the wheel. There were a couple more floor lamps throughout the large living room, but tonight they were not lit.

"I'll get you a glass of wine."

I wasn't sure what to do while he was gone, so I got up and walked toward the back wall of windows. It was dark outside, so I couldn't see the pond, but the coolness of the glass windows helped to calm me down.

"Here."

I turned and took the glass from Garrett. I noticed he didn't have anything to drink. "Aren't you going to have a glass?" I asked, taking a long drink to calm my nerves.

"I'm on call tonight. I may have to move quickly if I hear back on a question I have floating out there," Garrett said.

"What question?" I couldn't help myself.

He smiled at me, took the glass from my hand, and set it down on a nearby end table. He walked slowly back to me, his eyes never leaving mine. The spit dried up in my mouth.

One of his hands grabbed my waist and pulled me to him, while the other slid through my hair to cup the back of my head. The pressure of his mouth on mine left me dizzy.

Garrett pulled away from me, panting slightly. He didn't say anything, just stared at me as he ran his shaking hands through his hair. "I think we should head out to Paige's before things get so far out of control there will be no turning back."

I put on a fake smile, walked past him, and grabbed my wine from the table. I drank it in one gulp. "Ready when you are."

The ride to Paige's place was silent. I had too much on my mind to carry on a conversation.

Paige opened her front door while we were still in the driveway. "I was beginning to wonder what happened to you two. I almost…" She trailed off as she took in my appearance. Her eyes widened and she giggled.

I tried giving her the evil eye so she'd shut her mouth, but she just waved me off. Looping her arms through Garrett's, she all but pushed him into the kitchen. "Matt's in there. We'll be in in a sec." She gave him a gentle shove then turned back to me.

"Don't!" I hissed, hoping Garrett was out of earshot before she went psycho.

She quietly squealed as she raced back to me. "Dish! Your hair is really poofy, and your lips are totally swollen."

I touched my mouth. I thought the tingling was just my imagination. "It was amazing!" I blurted. I couldn't help myself.

"I knew it would be. C'mon, let's go find our boys."

Garrett and I ended up staying for about an hour. Between bites of the delicious lava cake, and glasses of champagne for Paige and me, we talked about the upcoming wedding.

Garrett caught my eye on my second yawn. Smiling, he leaned over and whispered in my ear. "I don't want you falling asleep on me. I do have plans for us before I head back to the office tonight."

Just when I was afraid I'd melt into a puddle on the floor, I heard his phone go off. Garrett looked at the number and sobered. "I need to take this. I'll be right back."

I looked over at Paige. I knew this was probably the call he was waiting for. How could I "accidentally" overhear the conversation? I looked down at our empty plates and glasses. I had an idea.

Paige must have known what I was going to do, because she reached over and helped me stack up all the plates. Picking up the dishes, I quietly tiptoed into the kitchen where Garrett had wandered when he took his call.

He had his back to me, which I figured was a plus. It allowed me to eavesdrop without him knowing.

"You're sure it's ketamine?" There was a pause. "Okay, that's what I figured. Can you tell how it's being administered?" There was another pause. "Okay. Thanks again for getting back to me so quickly." He ended the conversation, his back still to me. "Did you get all that, Sin?"

How did he know I was here? I made sure I hadn't made a peep as I entered the kitchen. Before I could figure out what to do, he turned around and slid his phone back into his front pocket. "I saw your reflection in the window."

"I didn't mean to hear," I said. A hollow lie, even to my own ears.

He didn't say anything, just smiled. "Uh huh. So now you know what I've suspected. Seems the victims were given ketamine, which explains how they were able to be easily manipulated and didn't put up a fight."

"I did notice the dishes at every scene. Two mugs. Sometimes plates and silverware, but always two washed mugs."

"I noticed them, too. We ran tests for fingerprints and DNA...nothing."

I briefly wondered how hard it was to come by a bottle of ketamine. Did it even come in a bottle? I had no idea what it was or how it came, but I was determined to find out.

Before I could ask any more questions, Garrett guided me out of the kitchen and back into the living room where Matt and Paige were snuggling.

Garrett handed me my purse. "We should probably head out. Give you two some alone time."

Matt and Paige stood up and walked us to the door. Paige gave me a little hug and whispered, "Call me tomorrow and tell me what you heard in the kitchen."

* * *

Wednesday was a dedicated office day. I called Paige and told her to meet me there. I knew she'd been looking up paralytics online, but now that I knew it was ketamine, I wanted to make sure she was in from the beginning. I hoped Hank was gone so I didn't have to make up some lie as to why I was on the computer and not out "doing my job" as he liked to tell me.

I threw on a pair of black leggings, a gray and white tunic sweater, and my black boots. I pulled my hair back into a high ponytail, brushed my teeth, and just like every morning ran out the door, blowing Miss Molly a kiss.

I called Mindy on her cell. "Hey, Ryli. How's it going?"

"Good. I'm calling to see if Hank is in?"

"He's out until this afternoon," Mindy said. "He's covering the grand opening of the new quilt shop this morning."

"Oh, no! I forgot I was supposed to go out there and take pictures this morning."

Mindy laughed. "He figured you were knee-deep in the murder and decided to cover for you."

I was actually excited about the opening of the quilt shop in town. It was supposed to be one of the largest shops in Northwest Missouri, and the fact it was coming to our little town was exciting news. If I had to guess, I'd say Mom was ready to run down there and buy material to start on a baby blanket now that Matt and Paige were getting married.

I picked up Aunt Shirley a few minutes later and headed to the office. We made a quick stop at the grocery store to pick up some fresh, homemade donuts to go with the coffee.

The first thing I needed to do was find out all I could about ketamine. I put Paige and Mindy on research. Who could get their hands on the drug? How would they go about getting their hands on the stuff? How was it administered? And how much of a dose was needed to incapacitate someone?

"In honor of all the marriages and hanky-panky that's being thrown around in this room," Aunt Shirley said as she started pulling donuts out of the grocery bag, "I decided to get commemorative donuts."

She tossed a small bag to each of us. I looked in and groaned.

"That's right. I got you donut *hoes!*" Aunt Shirley slapped herself on the leg, her body convulsing with laughter. "Get it...donut *hoes*...because y'all are —"

"We get it!" I cried. "You've lost your speaking privileges for the next half hour."

"Worth it!" Aunt Shirley said as she popped a donut hole into her mouth and chewed.

I gave Aunt Shirley the assignment to look over all my notes of the two crime scenes and start putting pieces together. I figured the former private eye would be able to see things we couldn't. And it would keep her quiet for a while.

That left me with the task of making a list of all the people I'd been in contact with over the last week. By the time I'd finished I had close to forty people.

"How're you doing over there, Ryli?" Paige asked.

I looked up from my list. "It's scary to think that one of these people has already killed two people and is now bent on terrorizing me."

"Ain't no one gonna get to you," Aunt Shirley said, looking up from her notes. "We'll make sure of that."

I hoped she was right.

"Wanna hear what I've found?" Paige asked.

Setting my list down on the desk, I gave her my full attention. "Let's hear it."

"Okay. We pretty much know ketamine is a paralytic...a neuromuscular agent. It can be used on humans and animals. From what I've read," Paige said, "in order for the killer to have that much control over the victims, they'd have to have ingested about one hundred twenty-five milligrams of the ketamine."

Aunt Shirley whistled. "Sounds like that's a whole lotta drug for one person."

"How do you think they're ingesting it?" Mindy asked.

Paige nibbled on her lower lip. "I think it's in a powder form. From everything I've read, it's the best way to disguise the flavor. The research said that the liquid form has a very bad taste that's hard to cover up. So my guess is it's in powder form."

I thought about that for a second. It actually made perfect sense. "I bet that's why there's always food and drink around. The killer is putting the powder in the drinks or food or something."

"Can you put it in food?" Mindy asked.

Aunt Shirley and Paige shrugged their shoulders.

I had no idea, either. But I was pretty sure Paige could find out with a little more research.

"What about people who use this drug or can get their hands on this drug?" I asked.

Paige's eyes lit up. "Illegally, there's no way to pinpoint. But legally, you're looking at your doctors, anesthesiologists, veterinarians, dentists. Maybe even nurses, I don't know."

My heart suddenly did double time. "Does this mean we can narrow my list down?" I asked, ruffling the paper in my hand.

Aunt Shirley stood up, pacing back and forth. No one said anything, we just watched her. I could practically see the wheels turning in her head as she moved stealthfully across the Berber carpet.

"I don't know if we can," Aunt Shirley said. "Even I know in this day and age everyone from kids to adults can get their hands on illegal drugs. If you know where to go, it's not that hard." She must have noticed my shocked look. "Hey, I watch TV. I know what's going on in this world. So, like I was saying, I don't know if we can eliminate random drug purchases. Or let's say it's stolen. How would we find that out? I'm not sure we can narrow the list down because there are too many underlying factors to take into consideration. But it does help knowing who originally has access to the ketamine."

I wasn't sure how. Seemed to me she'd just cut me off at the knees.

"Here's what I think we should do next," Aunt Shirley said. "I figure we're all going to the memorial service tomorrow. And everyone knows usually the killer goes to the funeral services—"

"They do?" Paige interrupted.

I was glad she'd said it aloud and not me. I didn't want to seem like an idiot.

"They do," Aunt Shirley assured us. "They like to see the torture and sadness of the families."

"Sick," I said.

"Anyway," Aunt Shirley continued, "I think we just watch. Look for anything suspicious. Try to surreptitiously look for people who are watching the reactions of other people. Maybe if we're lucky we'll see something or talk with someone that leads to a clue."

"I like it!" Mindy nodded.

I did, too. And I knew exactly which three or four people I was going to watch.

* * *

I told Mom I'd help her with the cooking and baking she needed to do in order to get ready for Dr. Garver's memorial the next day. Mom was on the committee at church that dealt with food preparation.

And, no, I was not on this committee. I was on the committee that cleaned up *after* the wonderful meal was eaten. But that's okay, because it usually meant I got to take home some good leftovers to snack on for a few days.

By the time we finished up at the office and I dropped Aunt Shirley back off at her place, it was mid-afternoon. I made it to Mom's house around three. She was already in the kitchen setting out supplies and ingredients. My mom usually takes the same thing to every church dinner we have…corn casserole and some type of fruit crisp, depending on what fruit was in season.

It looked like today we were doing a mixed berry crisp. I could see the blackberries, blueberries, and raspberries all thawing in a large aluminum bowl. When baking in bulk like this, Mom always did frozen fruit to help speed things along. Next to the fruit sat cinnamon, oats, stick butter, and brown sugar. I could practically taste the yumminess already.

I walked in the kitchen and Mom gave me a kiss on the cheek.

"Hey, Momma," I said. I know how much she loves when I call her that. And today I wanted to stay on her good side because I wanted…no, I *needed* a nice fruit crisp tonight before I went to bed.

"I think we'll start with three large vats of corn casserole, and then we can start on the fruit crisp after that. Hopefully it'll still be nice and warm for you when you head back home."

She handed me a pink and black apron with the words *Queen of Everything* embellished in white rhinestones. Mom was wearing her black apron that said *This IS My Little Black Dress*. I absolutely loved her sense of humor.

Once all the corn casseroles were finished, it was dinnertime. I started clearing off a place on the kitchen island while Mom got out the fixings for sandwiches. She had just finished making a sandwich when my cell phone rang.

It was Garrett. I could feel my heart racing as I swiped my finger to answer. I tried to tell myself to be cool, but I could hear the breathiness in my voice as I answered.

"Hey, Sin."

I smiled. I actually smiled at the nickname. This was so not good!

"What's going on?" I asked. I figured there had to be a pretty good reason for him to call me, during the day, on a day he was working. This was not like Garrett.

"I was wondering if you were going to be home later tonight. Maybe around eight?"

I wasn't sure if I should be leery or excited. His voice was giving nothing away. "I'll be home. I'm at Mom's right now getting ready to make the fruit crisp we're taking to the memorial tomorrow. But I'll be home by eight for sure."

"Good. I should have a little time to myself before I go back on call around nine. Can I drop by?"

Yes, yes, yes!

"Sure. And I'll have warm berry crisp to snack on. How's that?"

I knew he was thinking about the last dessert I'd made. I tried not to be offended, but it wasn't working. But I guess his hormones beat out fear of poisoning. "Sounds great. I'll bring vanilla ice cream. See ya later tonight, Sin."

He hung up before I could say anything back. Which was a good thing, because I seemed to be lacking witty comebacks with my tongue tied as it was.

"Got a boy coming over tonight, huh?" Mom teased.

A boy? Nope, a man. A man who could single-handedly tear my world and heart apart if I let him. A man who could make me respond to him in ways that terrified me. I was so worried about getting hurt...hurt so badly I didn't know if I could ever recover.

I must've had a terrified look on my face, because Mom suddenly hugged me and kissed my head. "Don't fret, Ryli. This could be a very good thing. And even if it doesn't end how you want it to, just remember...don't ever be afraid to take the ride. The ride is always the best part."

* * *

Mom and I finished the two pans of fruit crisp around seven. I stayed a while longer to help with dishes, which put me at my house around seven-thirty. Still plenty of time to freshen up before Garrett arrived.

Shifting the warm plate of fruit crisp into my left hand, I unlocked the front door of my house. Miss Molly greeted me warmly, weaving in and out of my legs as I walked to the table. It was all I could do to not trip over her.

"Silly girl!" I said, putting the food down on the table.

Miss Molly immediately jumped on the chair and stretched out her long, black body over the top of the table, sniffing the air.

"Get down." I gently pushed her down, glad I remembered to leave the foil on the plate. Miss Molly was constantly trying to nibble on human food.

I rushed down the hallway and started primping procedures. I plugged in my curling iron and took my hair out of my ponytail holder, shaking out the small bend in my hair from the rubber band. I then took out my sad looking makeup bag from the bathroom drawer. I always remember too late that I mean to start adding more to my arsenal of makeup. It never happens.

I decided to add some dark plum liner to the outside of my upper lid, and then added a little mascara. I had just finished refreshing my curls when I heard Miss Molly meowing. She was like a dog sometimes. She was good about letting me know when someone was coming to the front door.

Tonight Garrett was wearing his more casual police chief uniform—dark blue dress shirt and tie. While my stomach did rapid somersaults at the sight of him, my brain was smart enough to know he must have been doing something somewhat official where he wanted the uniform seen, but didn't want to intimidate too much. Was he questioning a suspect? It took every effort I had not to ask.

He didn't say anything, just held up the grocery bag containing ice cream, then pulled me to him for a kiss. Of course I went willingly. I'm not sure how long we stood there kissing, but soon I felt myself shivering. Believe it or not it wasn't from what Garrett was doing to me. The bag of ice cream was pressed against my back, and even through my sweater I could feel the cold.

"That's cold," I laughed. I took the bag of ice cream and started toward the kitchen, stopping at the table to pick up the fruit crisp. I got out the small bowls and ice cream scooper.

"Do you want me to heat up the crisp?" I asked. "It's not that warm anymore."

"No, it's fine." Garrett loosened his tie and took off his gun belt, setting it on the table.

I finished scooping the ice cream then handed his portion to him. Garrett took a large bite. I could tell by the way his eyes widened that he really liked it.

"You made this?" he asked incredulously.

I narrowed my eyes at him. He was not supposed to be surprised that I could accomplish such a feat. I was about to give him a piece of my mind when he corrected himself, "Let me rephrase that. It's really good, Sin. Once again you've made a lovely dessert."

I burst out laughing. I couldn't help it. When he let his guard down, he was a funny guy. It scared me how much I liked that about him.

I leaned on my tiptoes and gave him a quick, cold kiss.

"Playing dirty there, Sin," he growled.

I leaned in for another kiss when his phone went off. I waited for him to answer his phone. He swiped it but didn't answer.

"Alarm. I knew I'd better set it so I wouldn't be late getting back. I really do have some work I need to finish up."

Biting the inside of my cheek so I wouldn't ask any questions, I nodded my head.

Garrett retrieved his gun belt from off the table and fastened it. "What time are you going to the memorial service tomorrow?"

"I'm meeting Mom at the church around one-thirty since I have to stay later and help clean up. No sense in her waiting around for me. The cleanup committee and the cooking committee have designated parking spaces so we don't have to walk a long way with food. So I don't need to be there early like most people if they want a parking spot. If I have to stand through the service, so be it."

Turning serious, Garrett ran his thumb over my bottom lip. "Please tell me you're gonna be careful. I don't want anything happening to you."

I tried, unsuccessfully, to clamp down on the rush of anger I felt. Between him and my mother, I'm surprised they thought me capable of breathing on my own.

"Don't look at me that way, Sin. I just worry about you. I'm not too proud to admit I probably worry more than I should. You seem to have worked your way under my skin."

I felt a huge, dopey grin split my face. Standing on my tiptoes, I gave him a quick kiss. "I'll be careful, promise."

And I almost meant it, too. I bent down and scooped up Miss Molly. I knew things had officially shifted in the relationship.

CHAPTER 14

I woke up early feeling on top of the world. I threw on some clothes and headed to Mom's house. I realized for the first time since getting behind the wheel of the Falcon, that I actually felt like I belonged here. Like I could tackle whatever came my way because I was a smart, strong woman. Today I felt like I owned this car instead of it owning me.

I opened Mom's front door and called out a greeting.

"In the kitchen," Mom and Paige yelled.

Hoping my bounce didn't give too much away, I practically ran into the kitchen. Paige was bent over a Bride magazine, scribbling notes in the pages, while Mom was checking off items on a list.

I laughed at them. "Paige, you just got engaged. What're you doing already looking at books?"

Paige and Mom shared a chuckle, and then Paige gave me her best I-pity-your-stupidity smile and closed the book. "According to the checklist your mom is doing, I'm already behind."

"Ryli Jo Sinclair, what have you been up to?" my mom asked. "You look positively radiant this morning."

I did a little jig. "Garrett came by real quick last night, and as he was getting ready to go back to work, he admitted he had feelings for me! I thought maybe he did, but he actually said the words aloud to me."

Paige slapped her hand down on the table. "I knew it! What exactly did he say?"

I filled them both in on what had transpired. Mom gave me a hug. "I'm happy for you. I really like Garrett. I think he's just the guy to balance you."

Hmmm…what exactly did that mean?

To be honest, I didn't know what Mom would think about the age difference. We'd never really talked about it. A part of me was afraid she'd think he was too old for me and tell me I should try to find someone my own age. But after that little comment I guess I needn't worry.

I grabbed a blueberry muffin off the table. "Do I need to pick up Aunt Shirley for the memorial service today?"

Mom shook her head. "No. I'm going to pick her up. She called and said she'd like to get there in plenty of time to get a good seat. I hope you don't mind me picking her up instead of you?"

I laughed. "I don't mind at all."

I knew a good seat for Aunt Shirley would be toward the back of the church so she could survey people without them knowing it. It also made perfect sense she didn't want to rely on me to get her somewhere early.

"I better go. I need to run by the office real quick before the memorial."

Paige and I walked out together. I knew she was dying to chat but couldn't do it in front of Mom.

"I'm going to watch where Aunt Shirley sits," Paige said, "and then sit on the opposite side of the church one pew behind or in front, wherever I can find. This way we can see each other and everyone else at the same time."

She'd definitely been thinking about this. "Okay. Try and save me a spot if you can."

* * *

Twirling in front of the mirror, I decided I was happy with the outcome. I know it's probably shallow primping before a funeral, but I don't care. Knowing there was a good chance I was going to see Garrett had me taking a little extra care.

I'd decided on a black, long-sleeved body sheath that went to my ankles. I adorned it with my silver chain belt. It was a simple dress with a scooped neckline that showed just enough cleavage to be decent at a funeral.

I wore my one and only pair of heels. They were shimmery silver with tons of thin straps that crisscrossed over the top of my foot with one strap crossing behind my ankle. They were perched on top of three-inch icepick heels. No doubt I was going to kill myself in these at some point in the day, but at least I'd look good when Garrett came to identify my body. Being a practical girl, I also stuffed a pair of ballet flats in my purse for when I was doing cleanup after the service.

The church parking lot was already packed as I parked the Falcon in the designated parking area. I had thirty minutes to get inside and find Paige. I hoped she was able to save me a spot. I really didn't have the stamina to spy on people standing in strappy three-inch heels.

146

The parking lot where the food committee is to park leads right into the basement of the church. Opening the basement door, I walked into the large multi-purpose/kitchen area. This vast room could comfortably seat about two hundred people. At quick glance I counted almost thirty tables seating six people each. They were obviously expecting a large crowd to come downstairs after the memorial service.

I saw Mom arranging food on one of the large kitchen islands. I waved to her as I meandered around the circular tables to get to her. She looked beautiful in a black body-hugging dress with a black lace overlay on the upper bodice. I gave her a quick hug, anxious to get upstairs.

"Put your purse in Mrs. Pratt's Sunday school room," Mom said. "That's where all of us are placing ours."

"Will do. I'll see you after the service." I hurried up the ramp that led to the sanctuary, stopping halfway up to go into Mrs. Pratt's room and drop off my purse. I saw Mom's purse and jacket. I threw my clutch onto Mom's stash and headed back up the ramp.

Before I even neared the top, I could hear the dull murmur of a mass of people. And over that, the somber notes of organ music playing "Amazing Grace." The foyer was packed with myriad people and colorful funeral flowers. It was a slow process to the sanctuary.

"It's about time," Aunt Shirley hissed in my ear.

I yelped and clasped my chest. I hadn't heard nor seen her approach me. Now twenty people were staring at me.

Aunt Shirley snorted. "Cool your jets. It's just me."

"What are you doing out of your seat? Aren't you afraid someone will take it?" I asked.

"Nope. I'm sitting next to Old Man Jenkins. I told him if he saved my spot, I'd let him touch my boobs when we got back to the Manor."

I literally felt my mouth drop.

Aunt Shirley cackled. "Shut your trap, girl. Flies will swarm in! Paige is already in there, opposite side of me, one pew behind. The girl can follow directions. Now," Aunt Shirley said as she gave me a shove, "get in there!"

I stumbled and barely caught myself before face-planting on the carpet. I turned and gave her my best evil eye, but she'd already slipped through the crowd. Regaining my balance, I made my way to the glass doors that led into the sanctuary.

I was surprised to see just how packed the church was. I'd told myself it would be, but physically seeing all the people was jarring. Young, old, business suits, made up ladies, dressed down students. It looked like the whole town was here.

A slight exaggeration...but not by much.

The church sanctuary was set up in a traditional one-aisle layout with interlocking mauve chairs fanning out on each side of the aisle. I can still remember the uproar the chairs caused years ago. The old wooden pews were falling apart, the orange carpet-like fabric coverings were torn and nasty looking. When it became apparent something needed to be done, the church decided to cast a vote. Some members wanted to buy new pews, some wanted to put in the interlocking chairs, and some thought the pews in their worn condition should be good enough.

The chairs won out by a slight margin. There were still some church members not speaking to each other because of the outcome.

148

I actually liked the interlocking mauve chairs that lined the aisle. They were stylish and really soft. And when Pastor Williams got on a roll some Sunday mornings and preached a long sermon, believe me, you were glad for the added comfort.

The sanctuary could seat about two hundred people, and right now almost every seat was taken. Sometimes during the holidays the ushers have to open the glass doors and set up chairs in the foyer for the overflow. I'm assuming that's what they'd have to do today.

Near the altar a huge glossy picture of Dr. Garver sat on an easel. I was expecting the standard school picture. Instead, it was one of those cheesy Glamour Shots that were popular years ago. When I say years ago, I mean *years* ago. Garver appeared twenty years younger in this picture. I had to assume this was one of her demands.

A smaller easel to the left of the hideous picture cradled a bulky wreath made of different colored roses. The words "mother" "wife" and "grandmother" were woven within the wreath.

I saw Paige on my left, four rows up from the back. It must be that best-friend thing, because she chose that moment to turn around and make eye contact with me. Motioning me to sit next to her, I carefully made my way through the feet and legs of those already seated.

"I was beginning to worry," she said as I finally plopped down next to her.

"There's still fifteen minutes left before it starts," I said. "Aunt Shirley practically shoved me in here face first." I crossed my legs and smoothed my dress.

"Nice shoes," Paige said, giving me a knowing smile. "Very subtle."

I laughed at her comment. Unfortunately I forgot I was at a funeral and thirty people turned around and stared at me.

Oops!

"I brought a small notepad to jot down notes," Paige said as she showed me the short, spiral-bound tablet.

"Good idea." Why didn't I think of that? It's like I'll never get the hang of this private eye stuff sometimes. Even Paige is more prepared.

I tried to make eye contact with Aunt Shirley sitting on the opposite side of the church, but with so many people it wasn't possible.

Leaning over to Paige I whispered, "Have you seen anything or anyone suspicious yet?"

Paige looked over her shoulders, and then leaned over to whisper directly in my ear. "I've been thinking about what you said about the medical profession, and so I thought I'd watch Patty Carter and Dr. Powell for sure."

Exactly what I'd been thinking.

"Although I can't imagine they'd have anything to do with this," Paige quickly added.

Coming up with suspects was easy, but actually imagining them doing it was another story. I'd known both of these people my whole life. Both of them had never been anything but kind. But then again, rage made you do crazy things sometimes.

I spotted Doc Powell sitting four rows up from me to my right. I actually had a good view of his face. As wrong as it was, I couldn't help but think he looked good today. Very handsome. I really hoped he didn't have anything to do with the murders. I was still pulling for him to get with Mom.

Patty Carter was harder to find. I stood up, pretending to smooth down the back of my dress, hoping I could spot her in the crowd. She was sitting near the front of the church. There was no way I'd be able to see her throughout the ceremony.

What had she done, gotten here an hour early for that prime seating?

The organ music stopped, signaling the start of the memorial service. I quickly sat down and watched as Pastor Williams walked down the aisle, followed by Mr. Garver. His daughter was next in line, her arms linked through her husband's, as he led his weeping wife down the aisle. A little girl in a pink and white ruffled dress was hanging onto her mother's skirt for dear life. The Garver's son brought up the rear of the train.

And just like a train wreck, you couldn't help but watch, even though you didn't want to. I noticed the son didn't look near as torn up as his sister. Not that I suspected the son of the murders, but still…it was odd I thought. Or very telling.

As the family was getting seated and Pastor Williams was walking to the podium, I kept my eyes on Doc Powell. As Pastor Williams droned on and on, touting the wonderful attributions of the most hated woman in town, I tried to think of a reason why Doc Powell would want to kill Dr. Garver. Outside of the school board, I didn't think they ran in the same circle. I'm not sure Dr. Garver even had a circle of friends to run in.

Two songs, a standard mini sermon, and thirty minutes later, Pastor Williams was finally winding down. Only two people got up to speak when Pastor Williams asked for volunteers. I was actually amazed that outside of the daughter, I really couldn't see or hear any weeping. It was quite sad. Almost made me wish I could muster a tear or two.

The organ started up again, signaling the end of the memorial service. I glanced over at Paige, who'd been scribbling furiously in her notebook pretty much the whole service. Had she picked up on vibes I hadn't?

Leaning over to look in her lap, I almost laughed out loud. She'd been scribbling "Paige Sinclair" all over the paper—just like she'd done when we were kids. I grinned up at her. Shrugging her shoulders, she closed the notebook and smiled back at me.

I finally caught sight of Patty Carter's head as she was walking down the aisle to exit the service. One good thing about sitting in the back, you had to wait until the end to be dismissed. I couldn't help but note that Patty's face held no traces of tears. In fact, walking down the aisle, she'd periodically stop and chat with people…even laugh on occasion.

Guess when your archenemy dies, you can't help but feel pretty good.

Doc Powell also shuffled past us, head down. I couldn't tell how he was doing. I did notice throughout the service that he didn't seem to pay the Garvers too much attention. Not more than anyone else, I'd say.

When it was finally our turn to leave the sanctuary, I followed my row out to shake hands and exchange hugs with the Garvers. I wasn't prepared for the wave of sadness that washed over me when I came face to face with Professor Garver. I'd always liked him, so knowing he was grieving was heart wrenching.

I reached up and hugged him. "I'm so sorry for your loss, Professor."

A sad smile crossed his face. His eyes were bloodshot and hollow. "Thank you. Even though it's been a few days, I'm still in shock. I'm just not sure what to do with myself, you know?"

I really didn't know, but I didn't want to say that to him. "I know. Is there anything you need?"

Mr. Garver let out a shaky breath. "For someone to catch the person that murdered my wife. But that seems to be a miracle to ask for."

I said nothing and moved quickly down the receiving line. It was even more awkward with the daughter and son. I wasn't sure what to say, so I just mumbled my condolences and shuffled on.

When it was finally time to go downstairs to eat, I grabbed Paige and started looking for Aunt Shirley. I saw her talking with Patty Carter.

Weaving through the crowd, Paige and I made our way slowly to them. Patty turned to me and smiled. Correction...she grinned. Her grin was almost as bright as her outfit. I couldn't see what she'd been wearing sitting at the back of the church, but standing next to her now, I suddenly wished the ground would open up and swallow me.

There was no mourning black for her. Instead, she wore a dark blue t-shirt with the words "Today Will Be Amazing" printed on the front in day-glow yellow. She'd paired it with bright red Cargo pants and a matching red jacket over the t-shirt. The only subtle thing on her was the staple all nurses wear—Dansko clogs. These particular shoes were designed to look like Jackson Pollock had splattered them.

I'd always liked Patty, but today I found her to be out of line. "Wonderful day isn't it, Ryli?" Patty asked.

I ducked my head and mumbled a response.

"I was just asking Patty here how she found out about Dr. Garver's death," Aunt Shirley said.

"Usually I work the graveyard shift at the hospital. I was even supposed to be on duty the night she died, but I had to call in because I had the stomach flu. I don't know if it was something I ate or what, but I was pretty sick. So, I went ahead and started making calls to see if I could find someone to cover my shift. Luckily I found someone. It wasn't until probably six that next morning I started getting texts from people. That's why I didn't get up to Legends until later that morning." Patty turned to me. "You remember, Ryli? I saw you and Paige there that morning talking to some of the ladies about the murder."

I remembered.

I also wondered if Patty just realized she'd admitted she was home all night alone the night the murder took place. I was dying to ask her where she was the night Iris died, but I didn't want to overplay my hand.

"What about the night Iris died," Aunt Shirley said, obviously not caring if she overplayed her hand. "Where were you that night?"

Scowling, Patty took a step back from the circle we'd made. "Why do you want to know?" she demanded. "I don't have to tell you anything."

With that, Patty turned and marched away, her ample hips pushing the rest of the thinning crowd of mourners out of her way.

Dozens of bewildered people turned to watch her stride down the ramp into the basement of the church.

Well, so much for subtlety and not pissing her off.

"Seems we hit a nerve," Aunt Shirley chuckled.

"Yep," Paige said. "Seems to me if you're going to be happy about someone being murdered, you should be able to handle being accused of doing the murdering."

I laughed and gave Paige a fist bump. Rarely do I hear snarky from her.

We made our way downstairs to find a seat. I could smell the delicious aromas permeating throughout the church, and my stomach growled in response. A huge bowl of Mom's berry crisp sounded exquisite right about now.

CHAPTER 15

After thirty minutes of waiting in line, no sign of berry crisp or Garrett in sight, I was cursing my idiotic decision to wear the heels. I'd say my feet were killing me, but to be honest, I'd lost feeling in them fifteen minutes ago.

Everyone was basically smashed up against each other in the hallway leading down to the food. There seemed to be no rhyme or reason to the order, no line established, just a bunch of pressed up bodies waiting to get to the buffet.

I shoved myself off the wall and stumbled into Paige. Great, I was dizzy with starvation! Okay, a slight exaggeration. I knew it was because my feet were asleep, but it helped to grumble about the lack of food. I figured at this rate, I'd be passed out in ten minutes. The only perk in my future was the fact that Mrs. Pratt's room was not much farther ahead and I could run in and take off these shoes. Maybe I could even find a mint in my purse to tide me over before I expired.

"Careful there, Sin," a voice said, caressing my ear and making me shiver. "Hate for those sexy shoes to break your pretty neck."

My heart jumped as he brushed his hands up my arms. I tried to hide my smile. I didn't want to be grinning like a fool and have everyone see.

"Quit grinning like an idiot," Aunt Shirley said.

Garrett chuckled in my ear before turning to Aunt Shirley. "Aunt Shirley, always lovely to see you."

"Bite me," she grumbled.

"I can't stay long," Garrett said, ignoring my aunt's retort. "I just wanted to see you before I headed out. I know what you're up to, so I'm not even going to waste my breath and tell you to be careful." He leaned over to whisper in my ear, "And let me know if you find anything significant, please." I felt a light kiss against the underside of my ear.

It was a pretty bold move to do in front of everyone. But then I realized what he'd said. "What do you mean you know what we're up to?" I gave him my best innocent face.

Garrett narrowed his eyes. "You heard me. I know what you three girls are up to. I don't like it, but I can't stop it, either. So just be careful, please." He turned to Aunt Shirley. "I'm growing fond of her and wouldn't want to see her harmed." I'm pretty sure there was a veiled threat there somewhere.

Aunt Shirley must have heard it too. "Don't you worry yourself none. I'll bring her home safely."

Garrett stared her down, "See that you do."

He squeezed my arm, said goodbye to Aunt Shirley and Paige, and left as quickly and quietly as he came.

I watched him thread his way back up the ramp toward the sanctuary. I also saw Mindy waving at me just a few rows back. She looked smashing in a vintage 1950s hourglass-enhancing black dress. It had short, capped sleeves, a scoop collar, and a bodice that tapered down to a cinched-in waist. The bottom of her dress flared out from her waist and stopped just above her knees. I couldn't see her shoes, but I bet they were killer, too.

I hadn't noticed her or Hank at the memorial service, even though I'd looked for them. I waved back at her and motioned I'd save a spot for her when we got downstairs. She gave me a thumbs-up sign.

We moved forward again, and it wasn't until we passed the Sunday school room that I realized I'd forgotten to get my purse and shoes. With the throng of people still pressing around me on the ramp, I didn't want to go back up. Oh well, we were almost to the food and that was my primary focus. My feet would have to suffer.

Paige checked her text message again. "Your brother asked how everything was going. If there was anything new."

Matt had to work today, so he'd been texting every twenty minutes wanting a play by play of what was happening. Unfortunately, we had nothing to report, except for the fact we were still waiting in line to eat. Even the conversation around us was boring and of no use.

We finally reached the food, and I didn't even pretend to be a lady about my portions. I took as much as my plate could handle. I found a table that had been recently vacated by a large group. There was still trash on the table, so I cleared it off to make room for the five of us. By the time I finished, everyone was getting seated.

"So, what've you got for the paper?" Hank said, not even bothering with polite chitchat.

I rolled my eyes. "I wasn't aware I was supposed to be writing my article *during* the memorial service." I was always mindful of the fact he could snap my neck like a twig whenever the mood struck. Or discontinue my paycheck, meager as it was.

My stomach dropped.

I'd never ever *considered* Hank for the murders! He *had* been gone an awful lot lately, and I'm sure with his connections he could probably get his hands on drugs…but what would his motive be?

The look on my face must have been priceless because I suddenly became aware that the whole table was staring at me like I had suddenly grown two heads.

"What?" Hank demanded. "You're staring at me like you ain't never seen me before." He continued shoving food into his mouth without stopping.

Aunt Shirley must know me better than I thought since she started laughing. "I think Ryli here just realized you could be the murderer."

Hank stopped shoving the food in his mouth. "You ain't serious." He stared at me a little harder then started laughing. He laughed so hard the food fell off his fork. He laid it down on his plate and grabbed his napkin to dab at his eyes.

Mindy shot me a look I couldn't read. "Are you okay, Hank?" She placed her perfectly manicured hand on his arm. "You're scaring me."

Hank laughed some more, then patted her hand. "I'm fine, I'm fine." He looked over at me. "I'm not sure whether I'm insulted or impressed. Maybe insulted that it took you this long to realize I could be a suspect."

Mindy let out a gasp. Paige's mouth was hanging open, and Aunt Shirley was ignoring us, eating her mashed potatoes with gusto.

"You might just make a good reporter yet." And with that Hank started shoving the food back into his mouth.

* * *

Mom, Paige, and Aunt Shirley left around the same time Hank and Mindy did. There were only a handful of family and friends left. Most of us milling around were church members waiting to start the cleanup. Mom had brought down my purse when she'd gotten her things and set it on the built-in bookshelves along one wall. Deciding it was time to change out of the shoes, I walked to the sparse bookshelf and retrieved my ballet slippers from my purse. Sliding my high-heeled shoes off, I picked them up and set them next to my purse.

A hand touched my arm and I let out a little scream. "Thank you for helping today, Ryli."

I looked up at Pastor Williams and let out a shaky laugh. "Sorry, Pastor. You scared me. And it's no problem," the lie rolled off my tongue. "I'm glad to help."

"I'll just be glad when this day is over," Pastor Williams growled. "We need to move on. Get on with our lives."

I glanced sharply at my preacher, taking in his bloodshot eyes. He looked like he hadn't slept in days. His usually perfect appearance was cracking under the pressure it seemed.

"I'm sure things'll return to normal soon," I said.

"They'd better," Pastor Williams muttered as he turned on his heel and stomped away.

"Pay him no mind, dear," Sister Williams said.

I jumped again.

Geez, what is it with this family. They could sneak up on ninjas!

I smiled at Sister Williams, hoping she didn't notice my unease.

She patted my arm. "He's just still upset from Chief Kimball's visit the other day."

Wait...what?

Garrett had questioned the preacher? Was that where he'd been the other night when he came over in his uniform? If so, this must be serious.

I tried to sound casual. "Did Chief Kimble need to ask more questions about the Bible reference on the note left to me?"

Sister Williams's eyes filled with tears. "No. He asked Pastor where he was the night Dr. Garver was killed. We told him the truth. Thursday night Pastor had an early dinner, watched TV for a little while, and then fell asleep in his recliner. I remember going into the living room and waking him up around ten o'clock to go to bed."

"So he'd been in the living room sleeping all those hours, right?"

Confusion clouded Sister Williams's face. "Well, I'm sure of it. I mean, I was in the sewing room working for those hours, but I'm sure I'd have heard him leave."

Over the hum of a sewing machine? Doubtful.

"And how about the night Iris was murdered? Did Chief Kimball ask about that night?"

I saw anger flash in Sister Williams's eyes before she could mask it. "We again told Chief Kimball," she spat out Garrett's name, "that if the murder happened like they're thinking late

Sunday night, we were at church. I mean, we have tons of people who saw us here."

I couldn't help but notice how she was including herself in her husband's alibi. Like she needed to protect him. If he wasn't guilty, why would she feel compelled to emphasize she was with him all the time?

"Is that what they think?" I asked. Garrett had never told me the time of death for Iris.

Sister Williams picked at her lace collar. "Well, they think it was around ten o'clock that night. But Pastor is so very tired when he comes home Sunday nights that he pretty much always goes straight to bed. I remember that night specifically. He didn't even finish watching the TV program he had started. Poor thing was exhausted. I helped him into bed." Sister Williams turned and waved to some church ladies. "I better go help clean up. Thanks for sticking around and helping, too."

I had to admit I was stumped. It didn't sound like Pastor Williams had anything to worry about, but then why would Garrett be questioning him?

The committee put me on decorations duty, which meant I would be taking down and putting away funeral decorations. I looked around the enormous room to see who all was helping today. Usually the ladies on the cleanup committee did a rotation so the same person didn't have to do the same thing every time. I knew ten of the women personally. The other seven or eight I just knew by name.

We broke up into groups, and I found myself in the group that was breaking down the tables and stacking them on a large table dolly. Another group of ladies followed us, breaking down the chairs and stacking them on a large chair dolly. We continued in this rhythm for a while, stopping periodically to talk about the service or the upcoming Fall Festival on Saturday.

Cleanup only took twenty minutes with everyone pitching in. I was on the other side of the multi-purpose room, but I could see everyone was starting to get their stuff and leave. Hoping to grab my purse, some food, and slip out unnoticed, I headed toward the bookshelf.

I was shocked when I saw Patty walking toward me carrying a plate of goodies. The only people milling around were family and friends, and she qualified as neither. "Ryli, I was just heading out. I was hoping I'd see you so I could say I'm sorry for the way I reacted."

"What're you still doing here?" I blurted out.

She smiled at me as though I were a simpleton. "Oh, I was just upstairs looking at all the beautiful flowers. I dabble in horticulture, you know. I even have my own greenhouse full of flowers and herbs."

"I didn't know." Nor did I care if you really want to know.

"I came down here to see if maybe any dessert was left," she laughed hysterically. "Well, have a wonderful night dear. Enjoy the leftover food."

I watched her walk out the door and turn toward her car. She had it right—time to grab my stuff and head out. A nice glass of wine with some leftovers, maybe a hot bubble bath...I'd love to soak my aching feet. Yes, it was going to be a good night. It would be a perfect night if I heard from Garrett.

I was shocked when I saw three plates heaped with food, wrapped in Saran Wrap, with my name on them. They were placed next to my shoes and purse. I looked around, hoping to see who'd set it there. I noticed a group of ladies by one of the kitchen islands. Gathering my stuff, I went to investigate.

"Ryli, thank you for helping us out today," Mrs. Johnson said. "It always goes faster when young people help out."

I smiled at the group of elderly ladies. "No problem. Glad to help."

Mrs. Evans patted my food-filled arms. "Such a good girl. Just like her mother."

"Ummm…I'm wondering, who left the plate of food with my name on it over by the bookshelf?" I asked.

Mrs. Evans's face scrunched up, thinking back. "Well, I'm not sure. Maybe Mrs. Nelson. Why, is there a problem?"

"Oh no," I shook my head quickly, hoping to dispel any anxiety. "I just wanted to thank them. I didn't know anyone knew where my stuff was sitting."

Mrs. Johnson giggled. "Ryli, those shoes aren't to be missed. Everyone knew where your stuff was."

I felt my face heat with her obvious explanation. "Well, thank her for me please."

Mrs. Evans snickered. "She left a little while ago, but we will. You have a nice evening, Ryli." The last part was said with a wide knowing grin on her face.

Oh, brother! These women thought I was going home to Garrett. While that's exactly what I was hoping would happen someday, I didn't think it would be obvious to everyone else. I mumbled my goodbyes and practically sprinted out the church door.

CHAPTER 16

Glad to be home, I emptied my arms of my food and purse on the table. I walked down the hall and put my silver heels in the back of my closet. I didn't want to see them for a long time.

I changed into yoga pants and a tank top and piled my hair on top of my head. Taking off my makeup, I felt more like myself. Deciding to heat up the rigatoni with marinara I saw on one of the plates, I portioned some of it on another plate to heat in the microwave. I smiled when I saw the tiny parsley on top. Whoever had divvied up my food went out of her way to put an extra special touch on it.

I put the parsley on the table to eat later. Believe it or not, I loved parsley. While the food was heating up, I poured a small glass of red wine.

Hearing movement behind me, I turned and saw Miss Molly snatch my parsley off the table.

"Hey, that's mine!" I went to scoot her off the table and retrieve my parsley hanging from her mouth.

Miss Molly chewed on one of the leaves, breaking it off at the main stem. The rest of the parsley fell on the floor. She continued to chew as I snatched the fallen parsley off the floor.

"No more for you, you little scamp." I threw the rest of the parsley in the garbage. After I washed my hands, I picked up my plate and glass of wine and sat down at the table. Miss Molly was still eating her stolen parsley. The look on her face had me laughing. If I didn't know better I'd think she was trying to spit it out.

By the time I'd finished my meal and glass of wine, I was so exhausted from the long day I decided to skip the bubble bath and head straight to bed. It was still early, only eight o'clock, but I was drained.

I woke up to the sound of wheezing and hacking in my ear. Sitting up in bed, I knocked Miss Molly off my shoulder. Chuckling at how fast my heart was beating, I reached over to pet Molls.

"Silly Miss Molly," I cooed. "You scared me to death." It took me a few seconds before I realized something was wrong. Her breathing was labored. Switching on the lamp, I grabbed Miss Molly. Saliva leaked from her mouth, and the odor coming from her was putrid. I looked into her eyes and noticed they were dilated.

Screaming, I scooped her to my chest and ran to find my cell phone. In my delirium, I couldn't remember if it was still in my purse or on the table. Sobbing and stumbling down the hall, I reached out to find the light switch.

Light flooded the living room, and I saw my phone on the table. My hands were shaking so badly, it took me two tries to find Garrett's number and call him. I tried to calm my breathing as I waited for him to pick up, but I couldn't seem to think clearly.

"Pick up, pick up, pick up," I chanted.

"Hello...Ryli? I must've fallen asleep. I was going to call but—"

He must have heard my sobbing.

166

"What's wrong?" Garrett demanded, sounding suddenly alert. "Take a breath and relax. What is it?"

Taking a deep breath I told him about Miss Molly, about her labored breathing, dilated pupils, vile breath, and how she couldn't stop shaking.

"Miss Molly? Your cat?" I heard the exasperation even though he tried to hide it.

"Yes!"

"Okay. I'm coming over. Call Doc Powell. It's a little after ten, but it sounds serious."

I glanced up at the kitchen clock and saw he was right. It was pretty late, but I knew something was seriously wrong. I hung up and grabbed a cardigan to throw over my yoga pants and tank top. Sitting down on the couch, I continued to hug Miss Molly, rocking her gently as I sang to her. I knew I should pick up the phone and call Doc, but I was terrified to let Miss Molly go. I could swear the shaking was turning into seizures.

Praying Garrett would hurry, I got up and unlocked the door. Grabbing my cell phone I found Doc's number. Continuing to pace, I cooed to Miss Molly, telling her it would be okay, help was coming.

"Doc speaking."

At the sound of his voice I started to sob again. I knew I had to get hold of myself, but I couldn't help it. The thought of Miss Molly dying was making my heart ache in a way I didn't know was possible.

"Hello? Ryli? Your name came up on my caller ID, are you there?"

"Yes," I whispered. "Doc, something's wrong with Miss Molly."

"What's the problem?" he asked.

"Everything was fine up until the time I went to bed, but then I woke up with her panting in my ear, her breath stinks, she's shaking, her eyes are dilated. I think she's almost having seizures, and her breathing keeps getting worse."

Doc was silent for a moment. "I know she's a house cat, but could she have gotten outside somehow?"

I thought for a second, begging my brain to work. "No, no. She's always inside."

Again, Doc was silent. I wanted to scream at him to do something, but I knew it wasn't his fault. I felt Miss Molly seizing again. "Please, Doc, she's having another tiny seizure!"

"Did she eat anything poisonous? I'd think mushrooms if she'd been outside. It almost sounds like poison."

Poison? Where the heck would she get poison? I didn't have any rat poison or antifreeze anywhere in the house. I purposely didn't keep anything like that because of Miss Molly. I even got rid of my houseplants because I'd catch her nibbling on them when I first got her.

"Ryli? You still there?" Doc asked. "What about a houseplant or something like that?"

"No. I don't keep anything green because I know she'll eat..." my voice trailed off.

Ohmigod!

"Would parsley cause this?" I asked. "There was some parsley on the leftover pasta from the memorial service that I ate tonight. I took it off and set it on the table. When I turned my back she'd gotten a hold of it and ate one leaf."

Doc Powell was silent. Again I had to count to ten so I wouldn't scream at him. "Ryli, did you eat any of the plant? It's important you tell me."

The seriousness in Doc's voice had me nearly peeing my pants in fear. "No. Like I said, Miss Molly grabbed hold of it and tried to eat one of the leaves. Most of the parsley fell to the floor so I threw it away." I thought back to the look on her face. "I think maybe at one point she tried to spit it out."

The pounding on the door startled me and I let out a yelp. Miss Molly tried to lift her head off my shoulder and meow. It was so pitiful I started crying again.

"Ryli, open up!" Garrett shouted.

"It's open!" I yelled.

"Is someone there?" Doc asked.

Garrett barged through the door. "Garrett's here. I called him to come over. I'm so scared."

Doc cleared his throat. "Listen to me, Ryli. Put me on speakerphone, please. Garrett needs to hear this."

I took the phone away from my ear and put Doc on speakerphone. I handed the phone to Garrett so I could cradle Miss Molly with both arms.

"What's going on?" Garrett asked.

"Chief Kimble, I think Miss Molly has been poisoned. I can't imagine parsley doing this, but I guess it's possible. It's imperative you get out here now. I'll start getting the medications and IV set up. You just get out to my place as fast as you can. If there's any of the plant left, please bring it. But don't touch it. Sometimes oils from poisonous plants can contaminate the skin."

Garrett's face was like stone. I couldn't read anything. "Got it. Be there in five."

Garrett hung up the phone. "Where's this plant Doc's talking about?"

I pointed to the trashcan.

Garrett flipped the lid and looked inside. Luckily the parsley was on top. He grabbed a napkin off the counter, picked up the parsley, and shoved it in his pocket. "Let's go." He didn't say anything more until we were in the police-issued suburban.

"Where did you get this parsley?" Garrett asked quietly.

The fact he was so calm scared me to death. I continued stroking Miss Molly, her soft mewing was making my heart hurt like nothing I'd ever felt. "The church. It was on one of the leftover plates that I took home."

"Did you dish out the food, or did someone else?"

I thought back in my foggy haze and started sobbing again. I'd done this to Miss Molly. I'd poisoned my own cat.

"Ryli, I need you to focus. Did you dish it out or someone else?"

"Someone else. I found the food sitting near my purse and shoes. I asked some of the ladies who did it. Who had dished out my food. They thought it was Mrs. Nelson." I turned to look at Garrett. "The thing is, Mrs. Nelson is about eighty years old. There's no way she poisoned me on purpose, or killed Dr. Garver, or even Iris."

Garrett still didn't say anything. His eyes were on the road, but the lights from the dashboard illuminated his face, and I could see a tic in the side of his cheek.

"Was this the only piece of parsley, or is there more on the other plates."

Seeing the plates of food in my head, I was pretty sure this was the only piece. "I can't be one hundred percent certain without checking again, but I'm pretty sure this was the only piece." I wasn't sure if now was the time to say anything about my suspicions, but I figured it was now or never. "Since I knew the drug was ketamine, I thought I could narrow it down to Dr. Powell, Patty Carter, and a couple other people in the medical field."

"And let me guess, you questioned both of them at the memorial?"

"I didn't see Doc downstairs," I said.

"But your presence was noticed."

I didn't want to listen to a lecture, so instead of answering, I whispered words of encouragement to Miss Molly. Her only response was a lick to my neck. This tiny gesture bolstered my belief that she'd be okay. Relief surged through my cold body.

Please, God...please let her be okay. I prayed silently, repeating the words over and over in my head. I stroked her black and white fur, her long hair moved smoothly through my fingers. The rhythmic petting helped to calm my nerves.

"You do realize that it's quite easy for someone to get their hands on just about any drug they want, right?" Garrett asked. "Ketamine is not just regulated to people in the medical field."

I was saved from answering as we sped through the gate of Dr. Powell's clinic. The clinic was located five miles south of town on a gravel road, so we'd made excellent time. Doc's home was just twenty yards away from his clinic, so it was no surprise the lights were already on inside the building.

I'd barely gotten my seatbelt off before Garrett threw open my door and helped me down. I gave Miss Molly a kiss on her head.

"You'll be fine now, baby," I soothed softly. "Doc's gonna make you all better." Silence greeted me.

The clinic door burst open and Doc thrust out his arms. "Hurry! Give her to me."

I shoved Miss Molly at him, getting a sad sounding meow from her. A stab straight to my heart. Without a word, Doc turned and rushed her inside, yelling over his shoulder to come back with the plant.

Garrett took me by the elbow and led me inside. The sitting room was eerily silent. Usually it was a bustle of activity, animals weaving in and out of people, TV blaring, phones ringing. Now it was just a hollow shell...exactly how I felt.

"Stay here. I'll be right back. I don't want you back there in case..." Garrett didn't finish his sentence. He didn't have to.

With a sob, I sat down on one of the plastic chairs. Garrett handed me a tissue from a box sitting next to me. "I'll be right back." He leaned down and kissed my forehead. I nodded and sniffled into the tissue.

I didn't realize how much I'd come to love Miss Molly until now. I let the tears fall, not once brushing them away. I wanted to feel this pain as a reminder that she was still alive, that there was still a chance.

I'm not sure how much time had passed, but finally I heard the examination door open. I looked up and saw Doc Powell and Garrett standing in front of me. Miss Molly was nowhere in sight.

I felt another wave of crippling pain. I knew what this probably meant. I staggered to my feet. Garrett rushed over and caught me, wrapping his arms around me.

"Let me start off by saying Miss Molly is doing okay."

I looked sharply at Doc Powell. Had I heard right? Miss Molly was fine?

"How?" I croaked, my throat dry and painful from all the crying.

"Once Garrett showed me the leaf, and I registered Miss Molly's vitals and symptoms, I realized the poison she ingested was hemlock. A very nasty plant."

Questions bounced through my head. "How? How could this have happened?"

Doc Powell shrugged. "Hemlock is actually quite common believe it or not. Usually cats won't eat it. That's probably why she tried to spit it out as soon as she ingested it."

"She only ingested a little," I said. "How bad would it have been had she eaten the whole leaf?"

Doc Powell frowned. "It probably would have killed her, Ryli."

My knees buckled, and I would've gone down if not for Garrett holding me up.

"I've given her medications to control the mini seizures, ease her breathing, and reduce the gastrointestinal irritation she was having. I've also given her an IV, so be prepared when you see her. It looks worse than it really is."

I nodded my head, anxious to see her. "Can I go back then?"

Doc patted my arm. "Yes. Just know I need to keep her here overnight for more observation."

I nodded again and hurried toward the back door that led to the examination room. I heard Garrett call my name, but I didn't stop. I just wanted to get to Miss Molly.

I wished I'd have listened to Doc a little better. Sprawled out on a table, heavily sedated, a cast-like bandage around her back leg with an IV tube going to a fluid bag, Miss Molly looked downright pitiful.

I sobbed and rushed to her side, careful not to touch the bandage. I laid my head on her head. "Oh, little one…I love you so much. You scared me to death! You silly, brave kitty."

Miss Molly tried to lift her head, but the effort was too much. She put her head back on the cool table and watched me through half-opened eyes. "You're such a brave girl," I cooed, stroking her long hair. Her pink tongue darted out as if trying to lick me.

I laughed at her silliness and kissed her forehead.

Doc walked toward the table where Miss Molly laid sprawled out. I saw Garrett watching him closely, and I suddenly remembered what I'd said in the car about watching Doc at the funeral.

"I'm sorry," I whispered.

"Nonsense," Doc said, misunderstanding me. "You did good tonight, Ryli. You should be proud of yourself."

Garrett cleared his throat. "Doc, there are some questions I'm hoping you can answer for me."

"I can try."

"I know I called the other day to ask about ketamine, but in light of this new development I need to ask you specifics."

Doc's forehead wrinkled. "What do you mean?"

"I'd like to ask you where you were the night Dr. Garver was murdered."

Doc's face drained of color and his hands started to shake. "Just what are you implying here, Chief?"

"Nothing," I assured him. But I could tell he didn't believe me.

"It's just standard questioning. I've had to ask nearly everyone in town," Garrett said. "Believe me, I've come to learn that only tiny children are not suspects when it comes to who might want those two women killed."

Doc Powell sighed. He pulled over a medical stool and sat down. "I guess I figured eventually it'd get around to this. I can't say I'm surprised." He looked down at his wedding ring, twisting it slowly back and forth. When he finally looked up, his eyes were filled with tears. "It's no secret there's been no love lost between Dr. Garver and myself, but please don't make me tell you where I was that night."

I felt as if I'd been slapped. Was he admitting to killing Dr. Garver? Is that why he didn't want us to ask? I suddenly didn't want to know. I didn't want to find out the answers to this murder. I just wanted to go back to being blissfully ignorant, taking pictures and writing silly articles for the paper, petting and feeding Miss Molly every night...not worrying about dead bodies and body parts showing up at my house. I just wanted it all to end.

Garrett spread his legs apart and put his hands on his gun belt. "Sir, I'm going to ask you one more time where you were that night."

"Oh, now simmer down there, Chief," Doc said sternly. "I'm not saying I killed Dr. Garver. I just don't want to tell you where I was is all."

Garrett did relax his stance.

Doc sighed. "Fine. But can we do it in private?"

I whipped around to him. Now what was Doc saying? That he couldn't say it in front of me? Why? Was he with a woman? And if he was, why didn't he want me to know?

"It's okay if you were with someone," I assured Doc. "I mean, I won't say anything. It's been years since your wife's death. Heck, I've even been trying to set you up with my mom for as long as I can remember."

Doc's face turned red. It hit me like a punch to the gut. "Oh, my gosh! You're seeing my mom?" I almost jumped up and down with excitement.

Doc shuffled his feet and cleared his throat. "Now, I wouldn't say we're seeing each other...it's more like...well, what I mean to say is..." he trailed off.

"This is *awesome!*" I said.

"It is?" Doc said.

"It is?" Garrett echoed.

I grinned and clapped my hands, "It is!"

Overcome with joy, I reached up and gave Doc a hug. This man had saved Miss Molly's life, and now he was dating my mother. This man was the bomb as far as I was concerned.

"Well, let's just keep it between us. Don't tell your mom until I have a chance to speak with her, okay?" Doc asked.

"Sure. I mean, how can I say no to the man who saved Miss Molly's life tonight, right Garrett?"

Garrett looked at me, then at Doc, then back at me. He threw his hands up in the air. "Whatever."

Doc sobered and stared hard at Garrett. "Hemlock is a deadly poison. I'm assuming you think the plant was meant for Ryli and not Miss Molly?"

Garrett nodded. "It crossed my mind that this was no accident."

My mouth dropped open. "You think someone at the funeral tried to poison me? That's why you asked who made up my plate?"

"Yes," Garrett said.

For the first time in a long time, I was speechless. To knowingly be the next target of a killer was a scary thought.

I was so physically and emotionally exhausted by the time I got back into Garrett's vehicle, I knew I'd be out in a matter of minutes. "Thank you for being there for Miss Molly and me tonight."

Garrett leaned over and kissed me. "You're welcome. Now, I'm taking you to my place tonight. I don't want you alone." He chuckled. "And I'm not gonna lie. My couch is way more comfortable than yours, and I need a good night's sleep tonight."

CHAPTER 17

"Ryli, time to get up."

I turned on my side and pulled up the covers. "Just one more minute, Mom."

The bed shook with laughter. "I ain't your mom, Sin."

My eyes popped open and I yelped. Garrett was sitting on the edge of his bed, sipping coffee. He'd already showered and was dressed in his uniform.

We'd had a small argument over who got to sleep in his bed and who would sleep on the couch last night. I finally relented and left him on the couch.

"I have an interview set up in about an hour. I let you sleep as long as I could."

I glanced at his clock and was surprised to see it was already after nine o'clock.

Bolting up in bed, I tried scrambling out of the covers. Garrett put out his hand, stopping me. "I'm not in any hurry. Like I said, I still have an hour before my person comes in."

You can't imagine the torture it was not to be able to ask him who it was. I was dying to know how close he was to solving this case.

"I just got off the phone with Doc Powell, and Miss Molly is doing great."

Guilt slammed through my body. Here I was, thinking about solving the case first and completely forgot about Miss Molly. I closed my eyes and tried not to cry.

"Hey," Garrett said, "that was meant as good news."

"I just forgot for a minute."

He leaned in and kissed my cheek, then patted me on my leg. "Get up, get around, and I'll take you home. You can call Doc yourself from there."

He got up from the bed and left me alone.

I pushed the covers aside and walked over to his dresser mirror. Trying not to cringe at the massive bed head I was sporting, I bent upside down and fluffed my hair. Not much help.

I walked down the curved, wooden staircase and into the spacious living room. The glint of the wood from the natural lighting was breathtaking this early in the morning.

Garrett handed me a travel mug full of coffee, and we headed out the door to my house.

"I'll try and call or text once I finish up my interviews today."

Wait, now it's interviews, as in more than one?

Realizing I'd get nowhere quizzing him, I waited impatiently for Garrett to drop me off at my house so I could change my clothes and call Paige, Mindy, and Aunt Shirley. Garrett could spend all day interviewing suspects...I already had my suspect in mind, and it was about time for a showdown in Miss Molly's honor!

* * *

"We're sure about this?" Paige asked again as we were all four piling into the Falcon.

"Never been so sure of anything in my life!" I exclaimed, ready to get my beatdown on.

I'd picked up Paige and Aunt Shirley, and then drove straight to the office to meet up with Mindy. Hank was in Brywood, so we didn't need to explain our sudden disappearance. I called Mom to tell her about Miss Molly being sick. I conveniently left out her and Doc dating and how Garrett thought the Hemlock was meant for me.

I filled the girls in on what had happened to Miss Molly and who I thought the killer was and why. We spent the better part of the morning hashing out our plan.

After much deliberation, we decided to forgo contacting Garrett with our suspicions and capture the murderer ourselves. We knew he'd give us a song and dance about staying out of it and letting the professionals handle it. Then swoop in for the arrest, taking all the glory.

"Stop second guessing," Aunt Shirley snapped at Paige. "We all agreed. Now, let's go!"

I needed no further encouragement. And in honor of Miss Molly, I peeled out of the newspaper parking lot, spraying gravel everywhere.

Aunt Shirley whooped with excitement in the front seat, while Paige and Mindy huddled close together in the back. That image almost had me slowing down, unsure of whether or not we should move ahead without Garrett...but then I remembered how he laughed at the thought of us solving the crime, and I pressed down harder on the gas pedal.

Four miles out of town I came to the blacktop road that would take us where we were going. The house was only a half mile off the blacktop. A few seconds later, I turned right and drove up the long driveway. I couldn't help but marvel at the adorable mailbox. Instead of a standard black box on a brown wooden pole, this one had white chevron decals added to the black mailbox, and the pole was neon pink. Pulling up into the long driveway that curved slightly to the left near her front porch, we could see Patty's car.

I shut off the Falcon, and Aunt Shirley manually rolled her window down. "I probably shouldn't have had the oat muffins for breakfast."

We scattered like roaches out of the smelly car, yelling at Aunt Shirley the whole time.

"I'll take the lead," Aunt Shirley said, ignoring our outrage. "You three back me up."

She knocked on the door.

No answer.

She rang the doorbell.

No answer.

"Maybe she's not here," Mindy whispered behind me.

I was about to agree with her when a clanging came from the back of the house. Pushing us down the stairs, Aunt Shirley rushed around the back of the house so quickly, her polyester pants practically burst into flames.

Running to catch up, the three of us sprinted after her. I suddenly wondered if this was such a good idea anymore.

Aunt Shirley paused at the door of the tiny greenhouse. This close, we could hear sounds coming from inside. Reaching into the back of her pants, Aunt Shirley whipped out a snub-nose revolver that looked older than me.

The three of us started screaming.

"Who's out there?" Patty shouted.

"Now look what you did," Aunt Shirley hissed, as though pulling a weapon out of her butt is something we see every day.

Patty pushed open the greenhouse screen door, practically hitting Aunt Shirley in the face, and stared right into the tiny barrel of the gun.

"What the heck?" Patty shouted, scrambling backward to get away.

"Don't move a muscle, scumbag," Aunt Shirley demanded, sounding like a wanna-be Clint Eastwood.

"Well, now…this is gonna be bad," Paige whispered.

"What do you think you're doing on my property?" Patty demanded. "And pointing a gun at me no less."

Aunt Shirley waved the gun around like a madwoman. "We'll be asking the questions from now on."

I groaned. "Aunt Shirley, stop waving the gun around before you shoot someone!"

Aunt Shirley scowled, but not before lowering the gun a few inches. "Let's go, Patty. You got some confessing to do."

Before anyone could say anything, Patty whirled and took off for the back of her greenhouse. Without missing a beat, Aunt Shirley picked up a terracotta pot that was nearby and hurled it toward the back of Patty's head.

Patty went down like a sack of potatoes.

Paige, Mindy, and I stood there frozen…our mouths hanging open. Without a word to us, Aunt Shirley grabbed a rope off the ground. I looked over at Paige and Mindy, too frightened to move.

"Get over here and give me a hand, you ninnies," Aunt Shirley said. "I can't do all this on my own."

Kicking myself for thinking I could trust Aunt Shirley to do anything calmly, I helped her tie up Patty's hands and then sat her on the bar stool next to a long counter. Paige and Mindy stood huddled together.

Aunt Shirley gave Patty's face a few soft smacks, then stepped back and waited for her to wake up. We didn't have long to wait. A few seconds later Patty groaned softly.

"Open your eyes, murderer," Aunt Shirley taunted.

I didn't think Aunt Shirley needed to grab the bull by the horns, but this was my first interrogation, so what did I know?

"What did you four crazy broads do to me?" Patty said, trying to wiggle out of the ropes.

"Stop moving," Aunt Shirley demanded. "I said we'd be asking the questions from here on out."

"What questions? What're you talking about?"

Aunt Shirley held up her hand and Patty shut up. "Now, all we want you to do is confess and tell us why you did it."

Patty's wrinkled her brow. "Confess to what? What're you talking about?"

"Don't play dumb," Aunt Shirley hissed. "It's not a good look for you."

I heard Mindy chuckle.

Patty scowled at Mindy, as if trying to place her. Suddenly Patty threw back her head and howled with laughter. "You four have to be the dumbest bimbos on the face of the planet! You're gonna be in so much trouble when I get out of here and call the Chief."

I knew she was right, but then I thought about Miss Molly lying in the hospital. "You're the one that's in trouble, Patty. You may not have succeeding in poisoning me, but you did poison my cat. For that, I'm going to totally go ballistic on you. And you also murdered Dr. Garver and Iris, too."

I watched as a dark shadow fell over her face. "Yes, I hated them. Yes, I wished they'd die a slow painful death."

I could feel my heart racing with her admission. We had her. She was going to give us a total confession, and we will have solved the murders.

"But I didn't kill them," Patty said. "In fact, I just got back from an interview with Chief Kimble about fifteen minutes ago."

My heart stopped at that proclamation.

"What do you mean?" Aunt Shirley demanded.

"I mean, Chief Kimble had me come into the office earlier this morning to interview me. He asked me where I was the night both Iris and Dr. Garver were killed, and I told him. I also told him that I hated them both, but didn't kill them. Yes, I have a greenhouse, but I've never planted Hemlock, and he was more than welcome to come out to my place and see for himself. And as far as the ketamine went, what little we have at the hospital has to be accounted for, as Chief Kimble well knows. I'm assuming he believed me and had already checked with the hospital, because he didn't ask me anything else."

I'd listened to her rambling at first with hope of catching her in a lie...now I was downright fearful. I knew she was telling the truth. We had pretty much kidnapped and held a woman against her will, accosted her, and then accused her of murder. And we'd been wrong.

I'd been wrong.

I'd been wrong, and now we were in a boatload of trouble. We'd be lucky if we didn't all go to jail for a very, very long time.

I could feel myself starting to panic, so I looked over at Aunt Shirley for help. The way she was gnawing on her lip didn't boost my confidence any. I was afraid to turn around and look at Paige and Mindy. I knew they were probably scared out of their minds.

Patty's taunting laughter snapped me out of my stupor. I opened my mouth to grovel, to beg her not to call Garrett...I'd do anything!

"I'm not so sure I'd be that quick to call Chief Kimble," Aunt Shirley suddenly said.

"Why's that?" Patty demanded.

Aunt Shirley smiled. "I know marijuana plants when I see them. I'm thinking maybe we came out here hoping to talk with you, and next thing we know you are pulling a gun on us, and in order to defend ourselves we have to jump you. Then imagine our shock when we see you have marijuana plants all over. Well, being the upstanding citizens we are, we'd have no choice but to call the police—and maybe the paper while we're at it. Oh wait," Aunt Shirley smacked her forehead, feigning surprise, "we have the press right here!"

I heard clicking sounds behind me and turned to see Mindy grinning at me as she took pictures of the plants with her cell phone.

I practically sobbed with relief. Maybe my impulsive shenanigans *wouldn't* send my best friends up the river until our golden years!

"So how about this," Aunt Shirley said. "I untie you, we go on our merry way, and none of us ever mention this little incident ever again? And these pictures never get printed."

Patty stared at my aunt for a full ten seconds. "Untie me, then get off my property and never come back."

I ran over to where Patty was sitting and started untying her. "I'm sorry," I whispered, hearing my voice catch. "I'm sorry I thought it was you."

Patty stared at me with hate-filled eyes. I quickly finished the deed, then pushed Aunt Shirley and the others toward the door.

"Hey, Ryli?" I turned around and saw Patty reaching under the counter. "You're gonna wanna go a little faster than that."

Click-click!

I heard the chambering of the round before I saw the sawed-off shotgun being hoisted over the counter and aimed right at us.

Screaming, we all took off running, pushing each other out the door as Patty started hurling insults our way. I heard the door bang shut behind me and watched as Aunt Shirley and the girls ran full tilt toward the Falcon.

Paige reached the car first. Flinging open the back door, she hurled her heaving body inside. The impact had her bouncing around in the back like a pinball. Mindy followed her lead, and the two of them ended up in a dangled heap on the floorboard.

I could hear screaming and yelling all around me, but it seemed to be happening in slow motion. I heard the greenhouse screen door fling open and hit the side of the house. There was definitely some anger and momentum behind that shove. I dug into my pockets and pulled out the car keys.

I watched in amazement as Aunt Shirley leaped into the air and dove headfirst into the rolled down passenger-side window. Not to be outdone, I did my *Dukes of Hazzard* slide over the front hood of the Falcon.

I'd barely caught myself from falling on my face when I heard a loud *thud* overhead. Feeling bark hit the back of my head, I raised my arms to shield myself.

Crawling the last few feet to the driver's side door, I reached up for the handle. Suddenly I felt an explosion of pain.

"What the −" I screamed, rubbing my forehead. Aunt Shirley had shoved the Falcon's heavy door open and smacked me in the forehead.

"Get in, get in!" Aunt Shirley screeched.

Crouching low, I duck walked around the massive door and slid into the driver's side, closing the door. Aunt Shirley and I were on our bellies, nose to nose with each other, panting heavily.

"Don't go getting blood on my white leather seats," Aunt Shirley said.

"Nice swan dive for an old lady," I countered.

I put the key in the ignition and started the car. On a silent count of three, Aunt Shirley and I popped up into our bucket seats. I shoved the gearshift down in reverse and peeled out behind me.

I happened to make eye contact with Patty. Pushing down even harder on the gas pedal, I glanced in my rear-view mirror. I wanted to make sure no one was coming down the gravel road, since Paige and Mindy couldn't tell me. They were still screaming in the backseat.

I veered to my left, hoping to make a wide enough arc I could just throw the Falcon in park and peel out of there.

Crunch!

I didn't see the mailbox until it was too late. I'm pretty sure it was a total demolition by the look of horror on Patty's face.

I yanked the shifter down and shot off like a rocket, wheels squealing. I looked in the rear-view mirror one last time and saw Patty lower the shotgun.

Note to self...next time you go somewhere where you might have to jet, park with your hood facing the road.

"Mighty fine driving, girl!" Aunt Shirley exclaimed as she hit me in the arm. "Mighty fine."

I looked down at my hands and saw they were shaking, just like the rest of me I assumed. When I knew I was far enough away, I pulled the Falcon over to the side of the road and put it in park.

I turned and looked in the backseat. I'm not sure when they decided to pop up from the floorboard, but now Paige and Mindy were high-fiving each other. Like the last ten minutes had never happened.

Tears stung my eyes. I couldn't believe I'd almost killed us all with my stupidity. Where on Earth did I get an idea I could solve a murder?

Paige looked at Mindy and the two started giggling. Aunt Shirley joined in with her cackle. Pretty soon the three of them were wiping tears from their eyes and holding their sides.

"Are you all crazy?" I asked. "I about killed us and all you can do is laugh?"

Paige nodded. "That had to be the most exciting thing that's ever happened to me. I can't believe Patty Carter pulled a shotgun on us!"

"Well, speak for yourself," Aunt Shirley said, patting her hair in place. "I've had tons of excitement in my day. Although I must admit, it's been a while since I dove headfirst into a car window." She rubbed her right shoulder and laughed some more.

"Well, I've had enough excitement for the day," Mindy said. "I think I'll just keep my happy hiney at the office from now on."

I put the car in drive and headed back to town. I dropped Mindy off at the office with a promise not to tell Hank what we had done. I didn't want to get fired for almost killing his wife.

"What now?" Paige asked.

"Now," I said, "we just go home. Let the professionals handle this."

"We are the –"

I cut Aunt Shirley off. "No, we aren't. We are *not* the professionals."

"Let's just take it slow," Paige said. "I need to finish up some things for my mom and dad out on the farm, so why don't you take me home."

Aunt Shirley sighed. "And you can take me back to the prison. I want to look over my notes. Obviously we've missed something."

"Ya think?" I asked snarkily. I know it was beneath me, but I couldn't help it...especially since it had been my idea. I needed a nap and a drink. And not necessarily in that order, either.

After dropping everyone off, I drove the Falcon back to my house and parked it in the driveway. I was really surprised Aunt

Shirley hadn't skinned me alive when I hit the mailbox with her precious Falcon.

I got out and walked around to the trunk. Not a dent. I ran my hands over the fender just to be sure. Nope...this thing was like a tank.

I opened the front door and realized immediately something was wrong. Miss Molly didn't come out and greet me. The weight of the day engulfed me, and I started to sob. Walking to my bedroom, I emptied out my pockets, put my cell phone on the nightstand, slid into bed, and cried myself to sleep.

CHAPTER 18

The ringing of my cell phone woke me. I snatched it up but didn't recognize the number.

"Hello?"

"Ryli? This is Sister Williams. How are you?"

Sister Williams? My preacher's wife? My mind was still a little groggy.

"Fine. What's going on? Is everything okay?" I couldn't for the life of me figure out why she was calling.

"Oh, yes. Everything is fine. Your mother just left here. We're setting up for the Fall Festival this afternoon, you know." She said the last part as though I had completely let her down by not showing up.

How long had I been asleep? I looked over at my alarm clock and saw it was now after four o'clock. I think I said I'd be there around two or three to help set up.

"I'm sorry," I said. "It's just been a long day."

Sister Williams clucked her tongue sympathetically. "You poor thing. Your mother told us all about Miss Molly and what happened to her. Why, none of us here can believe it."

Thankful for the sympathy, I let myself indulge a little in the pity party. I knew it was silly. Molls was coming home soon, but I couldn't help it.

"The reason I'm calling is because I have something for you and Miss Molly. I discussed it with the ladies at the church, and we believe we have just the thing to cheer you up. We are downstairs in the church basement. Do you think you could come over real quick?"

No, I don't think I can.

But I knew if word got back to my mom that I told the church ladies I didn't want a gift, she'd probably turn me over her knee. She's always trying to get me to be more lady-like and genteel.

I sighed. "Of course, I'll be right there."

"Oh, thank you, Ryli. Just come through the basement. We'll see you in a bit."

Hoping to get this over with as quick as possible, I didn't even bother changing my clothes. I dropped my cell phone into my jeans pocket and whispered goodbye to Miss Molly.

There were only five other cars in the lot when I got to the church. I parked in my normal reserved parking so I could enter into the multi-purpose room downstairs. Not that I was ungrateful for the thoughtful gift, but I was hoping to get in and get out.

The normal core group of old ladies was just inside the doorway. A pang of nostalgia hit me when I entered the basement. The room looked amazing. The church had been putting on the festival for over twenty years. It was the same thing every year. The booths were always in the same spot, the same food always served. But that's what made it so special—the familiarity.

There were about twenty booths set up ready to go. There were ring toss games, a space for the cake walk, a miniature bowling area, and even face painting. My favorite booth was the baseball toss. I loved the old-time feel of it. The backdrop had a red and white checkerboard print, with old-fashioned wooden milk bottles. The baseballs were white with red stitching. Currently the balls were resting in shallow, wooden apple-picking baskets.

My least favorite booth was the balloon dart booth. While it was one of the most colorful booths, with about fifty randomly colored balloons attached to white pegboard, I hated hearing the popping of the balloons all night. It drove me crazy.

I usually ran the duck pond booth. It was safe and easy. Every kid got a prize, and I didn't have to worry about getting beamed in the head with a baseball or have my body pierced from wayward darts. The worst that happened at the duck pond booth was I got a little wet.

"Hello, Ryli," Mrs. Evans said. "We were just talking about poor Miss Molly."

Mrs. Nelson gave me a hug. "I told Chief Kimble today when he came over to interview me that I can't imagine anyone here knowingly giving you poison. I gave him a list of all the people that were helping put food away, but really anyone could have given it to you when we turned our backs."

Sister Williams patted my arm. "I guess no one is safe until the killer is caught. I just can't believe he was parading around at the service waiting to get to you. It's shocking."

My stomach dropped. I hadn't really thought about it like that. Had the killer been watching me the whole time I was people watching? Whereas I had no idea who the killer was...the killer obviously knew all about me and my personal life.

"Well, I'm sure your young man will wrap this up shortly," Mrs. Sellers said. Betty Sellers was the oldest member of our church at ninety-five. Her and her ninety-year-old sister, Mildred, live together just two doors down from the church.

"We better be going," Mrs. Evans said. "We don't want to keep you."

After the ladies left, Sister Williams led me to one of the islands in the kitchen. There were numerous cakes, cupcakes, and cake pops stacked on the counter, along with homemade caramel popcorn balls. Jugs of apple cider and cola were also lined up against the wall on the counter.

It was obvious a group of ladies had been here earlier baking, because the kitchen was still a mess. There were different colored icings, sprinkles, and even a little container of sugar sitting out on the counter.

I eyed the cake pops.

Sister Williams must have noticed. "You want a couple, Ryli?"

"Sure do!" I exclaimed.

Sister Williams smiled and busied herself gathering some goodies. She looked slim tonight in black pants and black sweater. If I didn't know better, I'd have thought she was going to a funeral. Her mousy brown hair was caught in a barrette on the back of her head.

"I told your mom and the other ladies to just go on home. I'd finish icing the cupcakes. I love icing cupcakes...it's so relaxing."

Whatever floats your boat there, Sister Williams.

I just wanted some sweets.

"I know how much you like chamomile tea. I've got a little left in the pot. I fixed some for the ladies earlier to help them relax for the evening. I'm sure after the stressful day you've had you could use it."

I practically wept. Did this woman know how to take care of someone hurting or what? "I'm just so thankful Miss Molly is going to make a full recovery," I said.

Saying nothing, Sister Williams finished pouring the tea. She then reached under the counter and brought out a sugar bowl. She dumped in two large spoonfuls of sugar. I didn't have the heart to tell her I didn't care for sugar in my tea. After a few seconds of stirring, she carefully slid the hot tea over to me.

"I prefer apple cider myself," she said and poured herself a large glass.

Blowing on the scalding tea, I took a small sip. I wasn't at all prepared for the taste...it had a little bite to it. I almost wanted to ask for more sugar.

"Do you know why I asked you here tonight, Ryli?"

I wrinkled my brow. I was pretty sure. "Yes. To give me a gift for Miss Molly."

Sister Williams chuckled as though I'd said something funny. Not wanting to say something offensive, I blew on the tea then took another sip.

Yep, tea's still nasty.

Sister Williams set an orange cupcake with candy-coated bone sprinkles in front of me. I'd never seen anything so cute before. I picked off one of the bone sprinkles and bit into it. It tasted like the stick out of a fun-dip. It was glorious. I gobbled up the rest of it.

I washed it down with another sip of my tea. I was just beginning to feel tranquil when Sister Williams started talking again.

Plop! Plop!

My cell phone sounded from the front pocket of my jeans. Not wanting to be rude by pulling out the phone in front of her, I carefully wiggled it out of my front pocket.

Great, it was from Garrett and he was yelling at me again.

WHERE RU? GOING STRAIGHT TO VOICEMAIL!

I'd forgotten it was sometimes hard to receive calls down in the church basement. I went to answer him, but my fingers felt funny.

I realized through my haze that Sister Williams was still talking. I blinked, trying to focus on what she was saying.

"I absolutely loathed that woman. The nerve of her coming over to the parsonage to tell Pastor she was going to push for our pay to be cut. She wanted to bring in a youth pastor to generate new blood. New blood! Who did she think she was?" I could see spittle starting to gather at the corners of her mouth. Her eyes looked wild and glazed.

It took me a minute to realize whom she was even talking about. Not only did my limbs seem to be tired, but so did my brain.

And just like that...everything snapped into place.

How did I miss this?

I tried thinking back to all the clues, but I couldn't make my mind focus.

"I knew I had to do something. One thing about your pastor, he's a wimp when it comes to playing hardball."

I willed my brain to keep up, but I could tell I was slipping.

196

"So I did what any loving wife would do when pushed...I killed her. Do you know she once told me that in business you couldn't have a heart when it came to doing what needed to be done? Can you believe that?" Sister Williams screamed in anger and threw her glass of cider against the wall. "Who did Vera Garver think she was?"

I watched as the juice slid down the wall at a snail's pace. Or so it seemed to me it was a snail's pace. I wasn't sure of anything anymore.

"So I made sure she understood what I thought of her ridiculous proposal that she typed up for the church board. It was so easy. I knew Professor Garver would be gone to night class. I slipped some sleeping pills in Pastor's drink, took out the bottle of ketamine I stole from my brother-in-law, and off I went to cut that woman's heart out!"

Her brother-in-law's ketamine? "Wait, why does your brother-in-law have ketamine?" I managed to ask. Or at least I thought I did. In my mind it came out clearly.

Smiling a twisted smile Sister Williams laughed. "He's a veterinarian in Columbia. I made sure Pastor and I went for a little family visit the day after Vera came to tell us what she planned. I went there, snagged a bottle, and came home." Her eyes suddenly darkened. "Of course he had the nerve to call me and ask about it. I told him it must've been stolen by one of the people at his clinic, and he should call the police. How *dare* he accuse me!"

"For some reason, Steppenwolf's 'The Pusher' is swimming around in my brain the more you talk," I sneered at her.

I vaguely remembered my mom telling me about that song some years back. I knew the ketamine was kicking in, because I could feel myself starting to drool, and it took a while to move my arms fast enough to wipe it away. At this rate, I'd be a goner soon. I needed to keep her talking.

I shook my head to clear it. "So that night you drugged your husband and went to see Dr. Garver, taking your special stash of ketamine. Then what did you do?"

Sister Williams reached out and pulled a huge butcher knife out of the drawer. She tapped the blade against the island counter. "I came and got this knife and the mandolin slicer. I went over to Garver's house, brought a nice dessert and thermos of hot tea already spiked with the ketamine, and pretended I wanted to understand her side."

I'm pretty sure I threw up a little when she told me about the knife and mandolin. I'd never be able to use a utensil from here again...assuming I survive the night.

"Oh, she went on and on about the good of the church, showed me the proposal she'd already typed up to present to the church board," Sister Williams's harsh laugh echoed off the walls of the room. "I plied her with the tea, waited for it to take affect like it's doing to you right now, then hauled her up on that kitchen table and started ripping out the heart she clearly didn't have! Then as a nice touch, I went ahead and sliced off her fingertips. Didn't want her to use them to write any more nasty letters."

You'd just hacked out her heart. Typing a letter would've been her last worry, you psycho!

Sister Williams laid her hand on my arm. I glanced down and felt my skin crawl. "Did you like my little present to you? I knew the minute you stopped me that morning outside Steve's Sub Shop wanting me to answer questions about *that woman* that you would probably snoop around until you found out the truth. So I knew you had to die. Jesus doesn't like snitches you know."

I blinked and managed not to laugh out loud. *Should I remind her Jesus doesn't like murderers?*

"Why kill Iris?" I asked, hoping to stall her.

"I was pretty sure Garver had ran her mouth and blabbed her plan to be rid of us to Iris one day when Iris was doing her hair." Sister Williams shrugged her shoulders. "So, Iris had to go. Of course, Iris *swore* she knew nothing when I went over to her house Sunday night. And even if that was true, she knew too much by then and she had to die. One less gossip to worry about. Jesus doesn't like gossips you know."

I snorted. *Who knew Sister Williams was freaking bonkers?*

"Figured giving you the very tongue that came from the gossipmonger as a gift would finally keep you quiet. Little did I know you were already fornicating with the Chief, and he'd come calling."

Fornicating? Who uses that word anymore?

I tried to clamp down on the hysteria I could feel bubbling inside me. "I thought Garrett questioned you guys and you had airtight alibis?"

Sister Williams laughed. "Silly girl. Your pastor wouldn't know which end was up most days. He's not really aware of this, but he's become quite dependent on my special drink I give him at night...sleeping pills mixed in with his two-finger measure of Scotch."

I'm not sure what shocked me more, the fact she drugged her husband every night or the fact my preacher drinks Scotch. I suddenly felt sorry for him. Unbeknownst to him, his wife was drugging him while she wreaked havoc on the town.

"It makes me sick to watch him drink the devil's potion. Jesus doesn't like drinkers, you know."

I couldn't stop the hysterical laughter that escaped me. I wanted so badly to ask her what exactly Jesus *did* like, but I knew she wouldn't hesitate to cut out my tongue. And I kinda liked having one.

"Then came the hemlock?" I asked.

"You were supposed to eat it, not your stupid cat. But you, your cat, I guess now I don't care. I just wish Miss Molly would've died so I could torture you with that knowledge while I killed you."

My phone plopped again. Another text message from Garrett. *WHERE RU?*

In her crazy ramblings, Sister Williams hadn't noticed the notification sound on my phone. Hoping to hide the phone, I hunched over and grabbed my stomach, moaning. "My stomach," I said and laid my head on my arms, surreptitiously forcing my fingers to cooperate and text a reply.

I lifted my head and noticed she was busy putting *more* ketamine in my tea. "This'll make it feel better," she assured me as she turned and set the container back on the counter.

In that moment I hurried and text a reply of *help church* and hit send. I think it actually came out *hep chuch*, but I knew Garrett would understand.

I wasn't sure how much time had gone by since my initial ingestion of the ketamine, but I knew from my research that it could take as little as twenty minutes for the drug to do its job. I knew I had to do something.

Leaning over the island, Sister Williams picked up my hot tea and brought it to her lips. I watched silently as she blew on it and stared me down.

"There, that should do the trick," she said. "I would typically toy with you a while longer. I love hearing them beg. But I have to get home soon. Preacher is expecting his dinner any time now, and he doesn't like to be kept waiting." She brought the cup to my lips. "Drink it!"

With all the strength I had, I lifted my arms and shove the scalding tea in her face. Her blood-curdling scream jolted me backward. I tripped over my feet and fell to the floor. Scrambling, I tried to stand. It took me three times before I could manage.

I glanced over at Sister Williams. She'd wiped the liquid off her face and was now sprinting at me with the knife.

Even though my mind was fuzzy, I could still remember where some of the games were located. I decided to go for the baseball toss. I remembered the balls were already in the baskets.

You know those terrifying dreams you have where you are running for your life, only to be running in place? That's what I was experiencing. In my mind I was an Olympic runner...in reality I was a snail swimming through peanut butter.

Hoping I could get to the baseball toss quickly, I took off like a rocket. Unfortunately for me, I tripped and careened headfirst into the duck pond booth. My head hit the lip of the plastic kiddie pool filled with water and plastic ducks. I fell to the floor on my hands and knees. The pool, which was sitting on a wooden platform, tipped over and fell on top of me. I was soaked.

I heard Sister Williams scream. "Look what you did to the carpet, you clumsy witch!"

Sister Williams was now practically on top of me. I shoved the empty kiddie pool off me and once again scrambled to my feet. The plastic pool hit Sister Williams's feet, tripping her up. As she started to stumble, she brought the knife down, inches from my stomach.

I'd always wanted a little work done, but not that way. Taking off once again for the baseball toss, I prayed Garrett was on his way. Hearing Sister Williams practically breathing in my ear, I knew I had to just grab some balls and go. I came upon the baseball booth and grabbed two balls without stopping.

Umph!

I felt pain radiate down my back. Sister Williams had taken my idea and hit me with a ball! I turned on my heel and threw with all my might. The ball stopped a foot from where Sister Williams was standing. I told myself it was the effect of the drug and not my lack of athleticism that had the ball falling flat.

Sister Williams doubled over, laughing so hard she had to hold her side. "You're pathetic! It's almost a shame to have to end your pitiful little life!" With that she took off after me again, knife raised.

I waited until she got a little closer and heaved the ball as hard as I could at her.

Smack!

This time the ball went a little higher, and I actually hit her...right in the stomach. I started to laugh as she doubled over again, this time in pain.

Who's pathetic now?

She stood back up, and I could see the wild anger in Sister Williams's eyes. She raised her knife-clenched hand in the air. "You die now!" She took off after me again in a hobble. Seeing a crazy-eyed woman with a knife hobbling after you screaming for your head kinda makes you take stock of your life.

I knew I had to wait until she was closer before I could hit her again with something. The drug was just too powerful in me. It was all I could do to lift my arms or propel my legs. I was so exhausted. I was also out of baseballs. I was almost ready to give up when I heard the distant wail of sirens.

He found me!

Either that or I was hallucinating. I'd read ketamine could make you do that.

Deep down I knew it was Garrett, and that little thought was all I needed to boost my energy and push on toward the dart board game. I saw the darts lying on the wooden platform and reached for them.

As my hand closed over the darts, Sister Williams's hand closed over my wet hair. She yanked me back with all her might. I saw stars and cursed. Yanking my head forward, I heard strands ripping from my head. I pivoted and braced myself for the impact.

Sister Williams careened into me going full speed. We fell headfirst onto the wooden board that held the dart players back. Spinning head over heels we both hit the ground hard.

Umph!

I felt the air leave my body. We'd landed wrapped in a tangled mess. Just my luck, the knife didn't plunge into her. On the bright side, it hadn't plunged into me, either. I still had one dart in my right hand.

Sister Williams wrapped her legs around mine and leaned over me. Knowing if she got on top I was a goner, I focused on her arms. She raised the knife in her right hand and brought it down toward my chest. I blocked her arm with my left hand and simultaneously plunged the dart into her neck.

Sister Williams screamed and pried the dart out of her neck. Blood dripped out of the wound, and I nearly passed out. Miles away I heard a door being knocked off its hinges. At least it seemed miles away.

I saw Garrett's face looming over me seconds before he hauled Sister Williams off me and cuffed her. He then shoved her off to Officer Ryan.

Now that the adrenaline rush was over, I was virtually unable to move. I just lay there, shaking uncontrollably.

Garrett knelt down by my side. "Don't try and move. Matt is coming with a board and we're gonna get you out of here. Did she give you ketamine?"

I nodded and lifted my hands to my face...only to have them fall back to the floor. It was like they weighed fifty pounds each.

Garrett reached down and wiped some of the tears and blood from my face. "I don't know whether to beat you or kiss you. I've never been so grateful to see someone alive in all my life." He tucked a wet strand of hair behind my ear and wiped the drool from my mouth.

Just my luck, the very heart-felt words I'd waited forever to hear, and all I could do was drool on myself.

I was dimly aware of loud noises and all kinds of ruckus going on around me, but I just wasn't sure what was happening. I saw Garrett look up and then Matt's face loomed over me.

"Mom's on her way. The town is already abuzz over this. Seems Betty and Mildred Sellers have been non-stop on the phone since they saw the police cars here and a shrieking Sister Williams shoved in a police car."

I tried to laugh at the description, but nothing came out. I closed my heavy eyes, hoping Mom wouldn't lecture me too much.

I let Matt take over and just tried to relax. Three other paramedics came over, and I felt myself being lifted, then raised, then pushed out of the church to be loaded onto the ambulance.

Crash!

I opened my eyes and managed to turn my head just a fraction. Amid the cursing and the screaming, I saw a 1975 Coupe Deville imbedded into the side of Garrett's police-issued Suburban.

Aunt Shirley jumped out of the car and came running over to me. "What in tarnation did you go and do? You weren't supposed to do anything stupid unless I was with you!"

I whimpered. It was the closest thing to a laugh I could manage. Aunt Shirley patted my hand and was giving me what-for when my mom came running up to the gurney.

I closed my eyes and wished to be anywhere else. I'd even take a lecture from Garrett at this point than have to face Mom.

She brushed my hair off my face. "Now's not the time for a lecture, young lady. But trust me, it's coming."

"You might have to stand in line," I said. I knew Garrett would want in on this reprimand.

Garrett crossed his arms over his chest. "You bet she will."

I grinned. Or at least I think I did.

The guys began loading me once more. I grasped Aunt Shirley's hand. "Whose car?"

Aunt Shirley winked at me. "Old Man Jenkins. I told him I'd let him touch my boobs again if he let me borrow it to go rescue my niece."

My eyes drifted shut. "Nice."

***

Pretty much everything else had to be wrapped up without me. I was of no use to anyone until they were able to stabilize me. The minute I was deemed okay, the rest of the story unfolded.

Once Pastor Williams was finally able to be roused from one of his drug-induced sleeps, Mom and Pastor Williams got into a knock-down-drag-out fight in the police station...literally. Mom knocked him down and then had to be dragged kicking and screaming off of him.

Garrett gave Aunt Shirley a ticket for hitting his police-issued vehicle. She promptly tore it up in front of him, claiming when an aunt was rescuing a niece, casualties of war were expected.

This prompted another ticket.

Hank, Mindy, Matt, and Paige were regulars at my hospital bed for a few days. Mindy, Matt, and Paige for comfort...Hank to harass me about the exclusive he expected me to have written and ready to go by print time next week.

I never really did get the big lecture I was expecting from both Mom and Garrett. I guess by the time they got done processing crazy Sister Williams, they must have realized I was lucky to have survived.

And for the first time in church history, the festival was put on hold. Pretty much everything regarding the church has been put on hold.

Once Sister Williams admitted to the killings and drugging her own husband, they locked her away and she's now awaiting trial. Pastor Williams resigned from the church and is in the process of moving out of the parsonage. Seems his spritely ninety-year-old mother wants out of the retirement home in Brywood, and Pastor Williams needs a woman to take care of him still. The church is trying to heal and move on with the hiring of another preacher. I just hope this one isn't as whacked out as the last one.

Garrett told me he knew it was Sister Williams the minute he got off the phone interview with her brother-in-law. It just so happened after he'd interviewed Patty and she told him hospitals and clinics have to keep track of ketamine, he started searching for recent break-ins and stolen ketamine. When a Dr. Williams popped up, he knew it couldn't be a coincidence and called Pastor Williams's brother immediately. His answers were all Garrett needed. He'd been on his way to the parsonage when I'd finally texted him back I was at the church and needed help.

Miss Molly was able to come home the minute I was released from the hospital. I'd never been so happy to see her. I hugged and kissed all over her. She meowed, jumped down, and demanded a treat. She was back to normal.

One good thing I could say about getting involved with the murder investigation—it gave me a taste of investigative work. And I really enjoyed it. If only I could convince Garrett how good I was.

✶✶✶✶✶✶✶

Ready for Book 2 in the Ryli Sinclair Mystery series, Girls' Night Out Murder? Just click here https://www.amazon.com/Girls-Night-Murder-Sinclair-Mystery-ebook/dp/B01ED34XQQ/ref=tmm_kin_swatch_0?_encoding=UTF8&qid=1566764176&sr=8-3 !! Happy reading!

ABOUT THE AUTHOR

Jenna writes in the genres of cozy/paranormal cozy/romantic comedy. Her humorous characters and stories revolve around family, murder, and there's always a positive element of the military in her stories. Jenna currently lives in Missouri with her fiancé, step-daughter, Nova Scotia duck tolling retriever dog, Brownie, and her tuxedo-cat, Whiskey. She is a former court reporter turned educator turned full-time writer. She has a Master's degree in Special Education, and an Education Specialist degree in Curriculum and Instruction. She also spent twelve years in full-time ministry.

When she's not writing, Jenna likes to attend beer and wine tastings, go antiquing, visit craft festivals, and spend time with her family and friends. You can friend request her on Facebook under Jenna St. James, and be sure to check out her website at http://jennastjames.com and sign up for her newsletter to keep up with new releases!

Made in the USA
Middletown, DE
25 November 2023

43358897R00117